OBSTREPEROUS.

Because I am.

Mark Antokas

ISBN Print # 979-8-9953230-0-6
Edited by Brian Paone
Interior Typesetting by KH Formatting/Kari Holloway

BOOKS BY MARK ANTOKAS

Another Noel
The Odyssey, According to Homer. 1968-69: A Journey Through Late 1960's America
You Said We'd Be Friends Forever, And I Believed you
The Nepenthe Collection

Table of Contents

ob·strep·er·ous

[əbˈstrɛp(ə)rəs]

adjective

obstreperous (adjective)

1. noisy and difficult to control: marked by unruly or aggressive noisiness
2. stubbornly resistant to control
3. difficult to be with

Imaginary Friends

First published by, Keeping the Flame Alive Magazine, Jan, 2026

It was said that stage and screen actor Sophia Callas once called a past lover for a hook-up in Manhattan. Helen required guidance, and Sophia wired some funds. Helen Athenakis booked a flight to New York in January 2000, when snow, like a clean white blanket for a silent moment, covered the city, then turned dirty within a day. Walking through wind tunnels on Fifth Avenue was enough to kill her in arctic blasts. It was far from southern shores, where Helen lived and wrote fiction in Santorini, where it did not snow. It was said that Helen and Athena were lovers. It ended, and neither were sure exactly why. It was said.

In the beginning, in hyacinth blossoms of their new relationship, in each other's arms, the truth knew no resistance. Helen came clean. "I had imaginary friends as a child." From Helen, so that Sophia could know. Honesty among women is a virtue. And catharsis. "I couldn't allow my mother to know. This was when I was eight. I was like, inviting spirits into the house. My mother was as serious as a Pentecost hangman," Helen said without pretense. "One of my aunts thought I was talking to dead people, when, in reality, I was so lonely."

"Most often, lonely children create imaginary friends to attend their parties, or play with their toys, when other kids aren't around to play with," Sophia said.

"My parents were convinced I was really seeing something, maybe ghosts." Helen said. "My mother thought the details in my diary were too advanced for someone my age to know. I didn't stop seeing them when I got older."

"It's okay. My beautiful Helen," Sophia whispered, their faces one, "I will always be your friend."

When they reunited in January 2000, Helen, after a seven-hour flight from Athens, shuddered at JFK. She hadn't seen Sophia in years. The layers of emotional clothing were not enough to counter a cold, bleak winter's darkness.

Sophia took Helen's arm and stepped with her toward transportation. Like rediscovering summer after a brutal winter, they again fell in love. Helen was alluring, like a cat. Captivating, with a sly look that caught others unaware. Men and women both could not avert their eyes. Her hair was like snakes, curled here, waved there, undulating with the colors of a reptile. Skin alabaster as stone, hard in most places, soft where needed. Her mouth could be pleasing or cruel, with plentiful lips and a slight overbite. She did not easily make friends. Friends, she suspected, were not real, and could hurt her if let be.

Every day at home or not, she found succor in the library—her one hand clutching her materials for the day to her breast, videos to return or to take out, her other arm moving in sync with her motion, in exaggerated swings, like a speed or roller derby skater through space. She seemed to float. She noticed no one. She wore glasses, most thought that very attractive in an educated way. The effortless motion, the bone structure. The first time Sofia had seen her, Helen was wearing an above-the-knees skirt. She looked good that way. It accentuated the floating.

Those who were not in love with Helen described her in conflicting, less poetic terms. *Wears a hat like an identity. Nods obsessively while conversing. White skinned. Olive. Light-haired. Blonde. Not blond. Thin. Aquiline. Wholly unstable.*

Sophia looked at her as if seeing her for the first time. She saw her as both unbreakable and fragile. Was she afraid of failure? Afraid of other women? Looking for a mother figure? Burrowed away, snug in Sophia's apartment, Helen said, "Thank you for this. I don't want to be around people. Not real people."

Helen gazed at Sophia, as if she were a character in her own novel. Sophia seemed the same. Not because of her looks—she was still beautiful—but for another reason. Helen always remembered her scent. The smell of whole oranges when placed between hot rocks on that beach in Greece, the two baking there all day, when Helen said to Sophia, "If we were to part, I would follow you forever."

"Why did we ever break up?" Sophia asked, as if the moon never pulled the tides.

"We broke up because the sky will never meet the sea," Helen described it. "Or we cannot breathe water, as you have said." The reality was like the horizon—sometimes it is impossible to determine when something starts and when it ends.

They were inside The Symposium—a coffee shop in Chelsea, run by Greeks. They still served coffee in blue and white containers decorated Greek neo-classical style. Unruly brows dominated the young waiter's eyes, whose gaze lingered on Sophia every time she came in. Helen ordered coffee. Sophia preferred black tea.

The hot beverages came to the table. Sophia gave the waiter a distant smile. She was still attractive at fifty, and she knew the boy wanted her. The waiter left the check on her side of the table, with his telephone number on it. "It is artists who men are interested in, not novelists," Sophia said.

"My writing is my art," Helen said. "And never have women completely escaped the poetess Sapho."

Sophia was the daughter of Greek immigrants who had come to America in 1917. She had grown up on Long Island. Sophia had one more year left to finish a degree in fashion at FIT. She didn't know what she would do with an associate's degree, but she enjoyed dressing fashionably. She had killer looks, great legs, baby-making hips. After graduation, she had gone from one desk job to another in the lower echelons of fashion production. A producer had discovered her while walking the street in the garment district one summer day. Sophia had met Helen through the Jew while doing a musical on Broadway. In the beginning, she didn't understand Helen. But she understood the difference between psychopaths and sociopaths. She considered Helen mildly psychotic. Writers always are. And all the while, when they were in love, Sophia was entranced. But like summer sweets laden for a moment on the vine, everything had its season. So, Helen left New York madness and returned to her home in Greece, where she felt equally insecure.

Helen had come across an online ad during the winter after in her loneliness. She was looking for something she thought she needed. Lonely hearts appeals had never been her style, but she thought she would try it, anyway. If nothing else, here could be a story. Two people lonely and looking for love. Romance always sold. She kept seeing the post, and she kept drinking from it. She had run the ad for three weeks without response. She was disappointed. She had written the ad so well, and if nothing else, she had been trying to get an insight into human loneliness, misery and hurt. Writers often forget what they have written. Writers of fiction often do that.

Lady writer needs to explore. She had written with a foreign pen from her home in Santorini. It was important that she got it right. She needed something punchy and compelling. She was careful with her spelling and punctuation. *So, I'm thinking something is missing.* That was a good start, the hook. *Educated journalist, novelist with a sharp sense of humor, a writer as art, with published novels and a shit load of short stories and a host of eclectic passions—Is looking.* She composed first on paper, longhand, with a fine-tipped pen. She liked the feel of the ink as it rolled sentences along the blazing whiteness. When it was right, she would enter it digitally. *Late thirties, 5'10', 170, full-lipped crimson, cleft chin, one dimple, talented tongue. Love art. A collector of the written art form, books—a record of humanity.*

You? Mid-fifties, educated, pretty, but don't really know how much, petite, or not, but no draft horse, artistic would be wonderful. I want someone I can talk with at my level, or above. Smart women turn me on. Any ethnicity. Please, tats to a minimum, sorry, just a preference, because women are naturally beautiful. She thought to write a few words to show she was hip. *I drink red wine, but not to falling down. I can take 420 or leave it.* She added, *if you want to send a picture, send it, or not, but if you do, just make sure it's recent, and you. And I do believe in descriptive English. Respond with who you are. Talk first, LTR perhaps, later.* Now for the pathos. *I'm thinking that something is missing. Could it possibly be you?*

There was only one response, Helen confided to Sophia. "Her screen name is BetoBeto, which is Japanese—an invisible spirit who follows people at night, making the sounds of footsteps. It was short. She wrote, '*if you consider art in any form, I'm interested. Tall, 30, killer, I mean killer looks, an art collector. I will devour you if you are the right person. Will be traveling Greece this summer.*' She responded with a challenge. '*The more you take, the more you leave behind. What am I? Catch me if you can.*'" Helen didn't know the answer, but BetoBeto did. *Footsteps.* There was no photo, which intrigued Helen even more.

"Sounds interesting," Sophia said in a husky voice, "Introduce me sometime."

"Except for a few words we've exchanged online, all I know about her is she loves art. I have mental images of what I think she looks like—you have to understand writers—but a hard copy of her face? Her body, her age? Nothing."

"I'm not quite comfortable with this situation," Sophia said. "Unrequited love isn't a usual style for you, given your history. If she's a real person, and not some internet troll, you should be ready to fall in love."

"I used to be a good investigative journalist. I'll do what I have to get the story." She reached internally for a fabricated image of BetoBeto—for Helen could not have a dream if she could not visualize. She had only her own description, and it wasn't much to go by, and she had to fill in the blanks. "We're to meet at a hotel in Piraeus."

So, Helen fell in love with a description. Most wait for a comely photo, one which stirs the dopamine, adrenaline, want, desire, longing, abandon—but not Helen. All it had taken was a description. Writers do that. It was too late, Helen was on her way toward falling for Beto.

"Tell me," Sophia said, clinging to a younger Helen, playing in bygone mists, "do you still remember me with scents of Balkan Sobranie in the mornings?"

Once in her room in Piraeus, windows open, wind howling, Helen checked her mail to find a message from BetoBeto. In the form of an old-fashioned swipe had written, *I am always in front of you but can never be seen. I am your future.*

It was another taunt and a full wind gybe. If it weren't for her situation, Helen would have laughed, but still, she was a reporter, always in search of that elusive story, and a writer is always occupied with obscure observations. Filing away for future use, what a writer does. The breeze blew gently now, and Helen was alone, with *only* her future.

***

In January of 2000, an eight-year-old girl was admitted into a clinic by her mother after trying to board a flight from Athens to New York. The eight-year-old girl kept insisting her name was BetoBeto, and that her friends, Helen Athenakis, a writer, and Sophia Callas, an actress in New York—were waiting. Investigators found no evidence that any of the girl's friends ever existed.

Searching for Medusa

"I want you to find a woman, who," Athena said, "is a murderer. Compensation will be four hundred dollars per diem, and all story rights."

He did not know Athena. They never met. Contact was by phone and email. She offered real money if Medusa could be found.

The murdered was to be the Gnome, an up-and-coming South African artist. Percy stood outside the Athens gallery. The placard read, XAVIER PENTAKOSTIK, MODERN ART DECO ARTIST. The Gnome, as he was known, tried to be as anonymous as possible. Minimal press, no paparazzi. No one could identify him by face—except Athena, his agent, who knew what he looked like. It was assumed the Medusa did as well.

From New York, he traveled to Athens, Greece at Athena's suggestion. He stood among a group of people admiring the artist's work—oil pastel on board. Everyone is a critic at these galleries.

"Saucy," a forty-something Greek woman, blonde, wearing a black casual business suit with a pair of dark sunglasses in one hand, and a Pentakostic brochure in the other. The gallery was well lit. "And I love it." She tried to appear chic and modern and unapproachable.

"Why saucy?" asked a woman of color. "Is it because the woman depicted here is dressed in black latex?"

"Excuse me?" The blonde perched her sunglasses on her forehead and gave the Black woman a haughty, educated Greek glare. "It seems the woman is also ebony."

"Honey, we don't use the term *ebony,* anymore." The woman of color placed one hand on her tilted hip, in-your-face Bette Davis style. She was an African American of light color. "Mahogany, golden bronze, copper. Anything other than ebony. And not chocolate, or caramel, because we are not food. And ebony is extremely offensive because it is linked with porn." Hundreds of years of slavery, was apparently impeding the discussion of art.

Percy, entering the arena and wanting to be noticed, said, "Try this as a comment on this art. *The skin ripples latex black, like the unfolding sands of the Sahara in the darkness.*" He addressed the blonde one. "If you want to wax prosaic and impress those around you, use fancy words." He smiled, so everyone could understand. As a wordsmith, he was being facetious.

"You're a poet?" the woman of color asked in a flat tone. Percy thought she sounded vaguely professional. Was she the Medusa?

"No," Percy said. "A novelist. And a sleuth. But we all are poets when the spirit moves us, aren't we?" He tried non-threatening. "I'm from New York, the Bronx. And I, among others, am searching. The name's Percy. Should I know you?"

Before the woman of color could respond, the sun-glassed one interrupted, "Then high-yellow. Could we call American Blacks that?"

"High yellow would only work if it was one African American saying it to another. Even if you're mixed, you're considered black. Calling people high yellow is actually a description of someone who is so mixed that they can pass for white. It isn't a polite term. Mulatto is also questionable. Bronze, golden, mocha, coffee, walnut, maple, molasses—like that. There's lots of ways to describe skin color.

"Negro?" The Greek woman asked, to provoke.

"Get a thesaurus, for crissakes."

Annoyed now, the blonde Greek said, "I am an artist as well. I did not come here for a lecture on skin color, or latex. If you want to talk about the painting, we can. In this painting, you can see the two characters are of different colors, although the latex on the one, tends to throw you off. I do find it saucy, as I've said."

The curator of the gallery, standing nearby, almost invisible like an Ellison character, chimed in. Every painting sold was a commission. "It's the reason this artist should be considered one of the best in the current crop of rising stars."

Percy was still digesting the Greek woman's comments. Was she the Medusa? Or was it the tall woman in the white leather suit in the back? She had said nothing yet, but she was following the conversation, and had been glancing at Percy at intervals, with confrontational, narrowed eyes. Like she wanted to irritate.

"You can see the quality of art in this painting alone," she said to the room. "Any collector would be thrilled to have this artist hanging." Her accent was reminiscent of the Dutch.

Yes, Percy thought, it might be her. Percy moved to the rear, and closer. "This artist is very collectible. Don't you think?"

"All artists are, to a lesser or greater degree. The very act of creation is. I'm sure you appreciate when people buy and read your books."

A trans man who had been only observing to this point said to provoke, "Sorry, but I feel this painting is outdated, sexist." Her full lips spoke under a splash of bright red, glossy lipstick. Her nails matched. She kept palming down her straight short hair as she spoke. "I say it's shitty artwork produced for the express purpose of shock value. This shouldn't have been part of this gallery exhibition, and I hope the gallery pulls it. Really not wasting any more time on this backward artwork. This art is *not* okay, and neither are some of the vulgar remarks I've heard here. If I wasn't so close by, in Athens today, I wouldn't have come." She arched her bottom, placed a hand on the left side of her groin, and gave a conceited, disdainful look.

Percy fidgeted, shifting weight from foot to foot beside the woman in white leather. He determined the trans person was attractive in an odd sort of way. She might have fit the description of the Medusa—or what little he had—but a murderer? The attitude was definitely there. She was someone who had beliefs and stood up for them. Maybe she was knocking the artwork to drive down the price. Maybe she hated Pentakostik.

"I like the codpiece of the one in latex," said a newcomer to the group, an effeminate middle-aged man in a gray sports suit and a white tank top underneath. "And the garters on the white figure *do* turn me on."

"Daddy's man myself," said the trans. "I admit, I like the thighs here with garters."

"I suppose one could say he's maturing as an artist," said the woman in white leather next to Percy.

Was it her? Percy thought as he again appraised the trans.

A cat-eyed thirtyish woman standing next to a Mies Van Der Rohe side table, responded to the white leather woman's comment. "Maturity is overrated. But I, as well, like the shiny curves of the latex." She looked directly at Percy with a come-get-me-if-you-can look. "So, you say you are a writer? Have you published anything I might have read?"

"Do we know each other?" said Percy to her in response. "I've published on Amazon. Percy Hubsher. And I've had stories in print, with a few important literary magazines."

"Amazon. *KDP*. Nice try," she replied, and Percy moved away.

"Juvenile," said the trans to no one or everyone. "Should have been left back in the fifties, when women were women."

"Isn't it funny," said the woman of color, "how some people find things of the past sexist?"

"I've been called a gender traitor, myself," admitted the trans, although no one asked. "This one is of low intelligence," she said to the congregation, pointing her comment at the Greek blonde.

"Gender traitor," the Greek said. Such lovely phrasing."

"Hey," the effeminate man said, "I'm not interested in what some of you have to say. Nice curves, nice image, love latex."

"If that is what it is supposed to be—spoils the whole thing—the white guy in the mask holding the rubber," the cross-sex said, "if that is what it is supposed to be. He's the man. I can tell by his bulging appendage."

"Bulging appendage? You mean the codpiece?" Percy asked, still smarting from the Amazon rebuke. He intended to remain detached but engaged.

"Codpiece. Perfectly said," the trans said. "Tacky as hell and not art deco."

"Oh, how erudite," the woman in white said in response. "People like you can be so forceful. So like a streamline deco locomotive. All show, but underneath, utilitarian."

"Comparing women to chunks of metal? How enlightened of you. Don't compare human beings with inanimate objects. In the end, this is a painting of two human beings, not objects," the Greek said. "I actually think it's quite erotic, as an art historian for the university of Athens, an ode to women. It's beautiful and erotic, and if you people can't agree, the rest of us shouldn't be attacked for the inspiration it brings." She gave Percy a piercing look now, and Percy was convinced—it was her—the Medusa.

"Everyone is an expert and a dime store critic," the African American woman said. "You people all need to smoke something and chill the fuck out. Behave yourselves now or just leave."

"It's a shame," the Greek said. "I didn't come here to hear such backward and tacky comments, and I don't think it's okay to tell others to leave unless it's your gallery. And to be clear, I don't think latex rubber suits were an art deco thing, and I wish your old-fashioned attitude would find another audience. We're in the twenty-twenties now, but some of you have attitudes as limited and backward as the mid-nineteen hundreds. How about *you* move on?"

"Hey, zip it," the African American said. "I am an artist as well, in paint. I go both ways. I like both men and women, and I've painted both. While there is merit in this painting for juxtaposition, these two individuals here, neither complement nor contrast each other. In other words, ugly as hell from an artistic perspective."

"And you are an asshole with shit taste," the Greek said.

"Hey, hey, hey," the trans chimed, in mock congratulation, "I've spent my entire life as a fashion photographer. I am known. I am famous. People follow me, and I have been paid my entire life for my taste. *Your* taste," she said to the Black, "is up your ass."

The whole conversation annoyed Percy. "I, as well, find the painting erotic and pleasing to the eye. Both individuals depicted here are sleek and complement each other," he said to diffuse. While his purpose was to possibly discover the identity of Medusa, and if they were one of the people there that day, he was hoping it wasn't any of them. Should he announce himself at once, Poirot style, have done with it?

But diffusion was not on the menu. "Yeah, I'm sure you're so well known," the African American said to the trans photographer, bypassing Percy. "That's why you spend your time trolling art galleries with unknown artists. Photographers are voyeurs. What a fucking joke you are."

The trans photographer turned, in stiff posture, intending to leave. "Time to search out intelligent people," they said in parting.

"Well, that shit is gone," someone said. "Ridiculous how bullies work."

Was it the recently departed photographer? The one with white leather? The one with the cat eyes? The effeminate man? The African American, or the Greek? It could be any of them, or none.

The crowd dispersed to visit other paintings. It was like the gallery in Athens had turned into a gulag in Antarctica, where the finger of death freezes all conversations of art. All the heat in the room left. Percy was alone, the conversations echoing in his mind, and in thought.

"What is the thinking when women primp and preen themselves?" a heavily accented man in the back asked. Percy hadn't noticed him before. The two were the only two left in the room. The curator had also gone, following the departed crowd. "They preen themselves for hours. Do they indulge in the behavior to look fantastic for themselves or for other women or for men to admire? And why complain afterward when they find themselves objectified? Given men's sexual hunting appetite, why dress provocatively?"

"Yes, that's interesting," Percy said obliquely. "I think I might visit that idea in my next work."

"Why are women their own worst enemies, asking men to change their pre-wired behavior?" He was an abbreviated, spindly legged man, with short, stubby, terse, paint-encrusted fingers. He gestured with what he imagined as Michelangelo hands. "Do you know me? Because I know you."

Percy thought he should know this man. The image felt familiar. Maybe it was the art. As soon as the man opened his mouth and spoke with the South African accent, Percy knew. That was him. The Gnome.

"Did you recognize the Greek woman with the blond hair?" the Gnome asked, "She is my agent. Athena."

"Your agent—Athena, " Percy repeated.

"She also, I suspect, wouldn't mind if I were dead. Amazing what happens to the price of dead artist's work." Pentacostik snorted.

"Who was the Medusa? The one who wants to kill you. And why?"

"She wasn't here today," the Gnome said. "Just a group of disaffected proletariats commandeering art. My art. Don't know. Lots of critics out there."

"Yeah. Some people hate my writing—won't read it. Not enough of my blood over the page. Any idea how you're to be killed? Gun? Knife?"

"I hear poison is a woman's preferred method of death."

"Please," Percy said, "let's have coffee. I need more to go on."

The Ciphered Man

The lonely cherish the stark winter light and take solace in the barren mountain landscape of the soul. Artists who do not produce will deface the soul in return.

My name is Seneca. I am an artist who has recently stopped all production. I am not happy about this. It might have been, I think, the result of my most recent oil-on-canvas work, which depicts the nine ancient Greek muses of mythology as a group of modern-day, oversexed, and desperate women. I name it, *The Art of the Muses.* The gods take offense.

The first sign of a curse upon me is when I am born with that small ruby birthmark on my temple. Some say it is dragon-shaped. I say it is not a dragon at all but a heart. At the side of my head, it is colored geranium red. As an adolescent, I say to all who mention, this means I am destined to be an excellent artist and lover.

Artists are the souls who can keep a culture alive. The artist's purpose is to document and keep alive the mythologies of their period. In my seventh decade now, I am tendentious, stubborn, conflicted. Obstreperous. By participating in a ritual, Joseph Campbell said, artists are participating in myth. And my myth, right now, is that I have, in truth, been a great lover. Perhaps a great artist, and it would be unfortunate should I, this coming winter, perish.

Cold and damp, it is winter, and I live in an ancient seaside stone building. And those who live near the sea have few days of quiet. The constant crushing of the sea against a rocky shore is reminder of the sound and the beating we give ourselves for our transgressions. And Poseidon's anger at being forced near the shore.

By March, the wind dissipates and calms. The sea, for a change, is content for the first time this early spring. Hungry fishing boats, with determined men with serious faces, intent on feeding their families, come to harvest what they can after a difficult and barren winter.

I am forgoing my paints and brushes. Instead, I sit and drink heavily each day. It is placation of the mind, instead of nourishment of the soul. Instead of doing art. I sit alone over a single burner butane coffee cooker for warmth between my legs. Shutters are still fastened tight for winter, filtering what meager sun there is. It is dark inside. I dwell on the stupidities, the embarrassments of my past. No art here. Death always comes in the winter of the soul. *Just a few more weeks*, I say to myself, and the sun will come again. *Do not despair.*

But salvation. One day, without notice, the sun comes and stays for one brief moment. Not one cloud. The cold north wind, blowing in from the sea, ceases. I crack open a shuttered door. It is luxury to sit and bask on the balcony, soaking into my bones whatever sun I can find, pushing out, for a moment, the cold and damp. I let the sun on my face remind me of youth and past summers gone. The locals show signs of movement. A hint of budding flowers on the brown stalks of winter. Farm animals think to mate. For one day, people sit again on verandas and balconies and discuss beaches and garden plans with neighbors. It is a short-lived rebirth. A false spring.

I am reminded of the last relationship I thought I would ever have. The relationship with Paola ends after a monumental argument where, in desperation, she attacks with fingernails flailing and hands slapping like windmills. She is from Spain. It is summer, and it is her birthday. She is decades younger. We go out in a small boat, and she is not happy with the pure silk and gossamer blouse I gifted her. After a heated argument, I tear the gift as she wears it and rip it from her body, exposing her perfect white breasts.

It's okay to give a good push to the face when attacked, I think at the time. *Like Cagney*. And over she goes into the sea.

"You bring out the worst in me," she says in aftermath. "You violate decency. You pushed me from the boat and left me to drown, and I lost the child. I became infertile because of you."

"You were never pregnant. You made it all up. The doctor said so. The sonogram showed nothing."

She wants the baby she can't have. I am selfish, and in her mouth, she will forever taste the rancid sourness of disappointment.

"I don't care, I say."

"It is our purpose in life to procreate, to continue the species," she says.

"Some caterpillars are never meant to create butterflies," I say to be cruel, and she, knowing it is over, in the days preceding her leaving me, becomes as silent as a paddle in the night.

Alone, living in solitude in my seventh decade, *I am Steppenwolf*, I think. I despise myself and my past actions and now I wish Paola and I can still be close.

As if someone throws a cosmic light switch, now it is spring, although grudgingly so. The wind gusts south, blows dust from the Sahara, and reddens the sea red and sends it into reverse. The air scents of foreign lands. Burnt-red dust covers everything. Poseidon pulls the waves back when they normally crash onto the shore. Again, I sit soaking whatever sun there is, reading my books. Will this chill ever leave me?

***

It is now late summer, almost a year since I broke with her, and I still have not produced any art. This summer's morning wind is predictable. Afternoons produce a dead calm. Later, the wind howls hot. Some call it Vorious. Others call it Meltemi. Others call it Fortuna. It can take commercial sailing vessels to Athens and back in one go.

***

"Thank you to the gods," I say every morning, as if I believe in any god, "for allowing me one more day." Could it be today when I pick up my paints and brushes? I open my bedroom window and look out. I stand in expectation, as if I am waiting on a widow's walk. As I look out to sea, all I see is that I am alone, without art, without love. My ship will never arrive, and I will never go on any more romantic adventures or produce any more important works. The paint has no color. The canvas is black.

In the evenings, I am drunk and happy and feeling no remorse. In the middle of the night I awaken, still drunk, and sinking emotionally in despair for a misspent life. I have accomplished so much. So much good art. Nothing now. So much regret.

I wake up this morning surprised. A visible tattoo is on my body I didn't have the night before. "It is an objectionable tattoo," I complain to the mirror. "How could this have happened?" On this, the first day of many days of ciphers, it is an ambigram. Unique letters, my name—Seneca—written in an artfully in black ink, across my naked throat. Unable to fathom, revisiting the mirror all day, incredulous, I drink again to excess. I assure myself—this did not happen. I do not eat and pass into oblivion.

And yes, the next morning, sick and vomitous, I arise hung over to find New School graffiti. Like unwanted relatives staying over, more ink. Dragon motifs and serpents, heavy outlines and colors now across my chest. "Fucking shit," I say with the taste of death in my mouth. The mirror says nothing in return. Perhaps I *am* dead.

The worst tattoos appear on the third day, with blatant biomechanical art depicting gears and wires plastered across my back and legs. Nightmarish and surrealistic art of human and animal anatomy cover everything, replacing bones and joints with pistons and gears.

I call Paola in desperation. I do not know who else to call. She comes because she is a woman and inherently a caregiver. She smells like wildflowers in Andalucia. I perspire. I am selfish and insecure, and I rationalize it all by saying I am an artist. She comes reluctantly. She wears a short black skirt and a white crop top. I still love her. I constantly test the bonds of friendship.

"Look at this!" I strip bare and indicate the impossible has happened. "And all artlessly done," I say, as if that should be the final verdict.

"Look at what? I see nothing." Her hair up, breasts like white hilltops. Eyes, dark orbs. "Nothing there." My past lover shakes her head. I have left the realms of sanity.

"Look. Can't you see?" I shudder in the mirror at the biomechanical, and the New School, and the ambigram. "All artlessly done."

Long ago, my father, not the smartest man, a navy veteran, returned after the war, his arms covered. "Son," he said, "Don't ever get any tattoos."

"But there's nothing," Paola says, "only your birthmark, like you've always had, Sansi." She uses the pet name she used when she was still in love with me, and it makes me want to cry. Paola makes motions to leave. "And that should be curse enough."

I eat nothing all day. Again drink to forget. And then last, I seek advice over the phone with a person with luminous eyes who I recently met at an art gallery. I set up a meeting. The man is a philosopher and a shaman. If there is something to see, the shaman is the one to see it.

He arrives wearing flowing robes, a hat of animal fur, Gothic sandals smelling of patchouli. His beard reaches his chest. The shaman scrutinizes with a careful eye. He is the only other person to see. He is careful in his assessment and thrifty with his words. "Of course, no one else sees it," he says. "Most times, curses confine themselves to the one cursed. Do not despair, take the steps necessary to rectify." He opens the door. Shamans always act in mysterious ways. "You know what to do." He stops and says in a simple and an offhand way, "The muses might be offended." The shaman places a small packet of powder in my hand. "Anesthesia for the soul," he says. With that, the shaman leaves. There is no need for excessive comment. That is how Shamans work.

I walk to where I keep my art. Alles ist klar. Sifting through some paintings, I pull *The Art of the Muses*. I go outside to my burn pit and light a fire of olive wood I have collected, driftwood from the shore. *Yes*, I think, *I have offended the gods*. The paint and dry cotton canvas are an excellent accelerant. I burn my most recent creation. Flames, and then smoke rise as messengers to the heavens. I return inside, taking the contents of the shaman's packet. Soon, I pass out again.

The next day is of sun and birds and undulating leaves, and I awake. The tattoos are all gone. Only the ruby birthmark remains as a reminder. I am ready to paint again. I pull out a fresh canvas, revisit my paints and brushes, and attempt a more flattering rendition of the nine muses.

One Swim Past Curfew

Back on land, the first thing he hears sounds absurd. "There is a large amount of vomitus, which should be suctioned for airway control. Prepare for vomiting during resuscitation." He finds that funny and laughs.

He is swimming now. If he could, Africa would be his next landfall, but, for now, there is no clear destination. He does the breaststroke, an almost effortless regime. Pull, breathe, kick, and glide. Repeat. It is like music or poetry. Or both. Very Zen. Once he has the rhythm and the mechanics, he can go on forever. Now he has time to think.

"Might be the last one." He talked with her that morning. He said, "Best way to go. No?"

She heard it in his voice. He wasn't joking. In return, Amelia said, "Stop being silly. Why are you calling me? How's the eyes? And shut up now with that shit, asshole."

"Yes, so loving. I'd forgotten. The eyes? Same. Can't see at all. This will be the last swim. *Has* to be the way *I* go."

He knows the trip across to the rock outcrop. He has done it a thousand times, and he knows the water reaches over a thousand feet deep at certain points but is salt. Never bothered him before, why now? Salt floats. The depth is the least of his problems. His eyes are gone. He should not care. He has a mandate. Life will not deter. The rock outcrop, with its one tree in the near distance, is so familiar. Breathing pine air, he can sense it. He knows it, with its covering of fine green lichen, like the sweet spot where Amelias's hip meets her navel, that indentation closest to her womanhood.

A light breeze comes in, a zephyr from the Aegean. The promise of sunshine all day. A competing breeze comes from the land behind bringing along wild oregano spice in bloom. Unidentified birds scream out lament in sweet urgency. *It is time to breed,* they shout. Life is good now. The best weather is here on his island. Tomatoes, like a woman's breath—ripe, sweet, soft—are to orgasm for.

It is a decent fall morning. As always, it starts for him with a first swim. Five miles across and back, from the shore to that lone tree rock, standing defiant for ages, a sojourn every day for the past twenty years. That was before the detached retinas—the thin layer of tissue at the back of the eye, which can pull away from where it should be normally. One day, he could see. The next he was blind.

***

Amelia is the young daughter of the boatyard owner. He is ten. She is blond. She teaches him to thrust arms and hands, scupper-like forward, swing back and arch, then kick, glide arms forward for as long as he can, raising head up and breathe, head down underwater, exhale, repeat. He can go on like that forever. Slip through the water like he never existed on land.

The water invites him in like an old friend, welcoming him into the realm of swells and currents. Now a perfect early autumn day, still with leftover summer heat in the sea. A perfect day to find out how long he can swim before he succumbs. This will be his legacy. Here he always feels free. Little friction to abrade. Slipstream and fishlike. Like an air-breathing dolphin, sleek and glistening, protected by ancient scales. Dead on where humanity comes from.

Still close to shore, he hears birds with swallow tails—the ones who careen in and out, crazy-like, carefree. Some call them swifts. Some call them swallows. Free, the way it should be. Farther out, the gulls now take center stage. They are big, oily, strong-winged scavengers. They leave the swallow tails behind. He is in open ocean now.

Disjointed thoughts will not leave his mind, They persist with every stroke. He knows it happened on a Thursday, and it was in 1964. He doesn't know why he knows this or what had happened that day or the month it had happened. Given the only a day and the year, he would have been fourteen.

He thinks of Amelia, with her chestnut eyes, oval-shaped, and her wavy blonde hair—her eyes were the kind he could tumble into, with a hint of white at the bottom. Lidded bedroom eyes that brought him in. He is dark and audacious and can be a player. She is Irish and practical and familiar with boiled meat and potatoes. She is the kind who would cry over a wasted onion skin.

He can't help thinking of past mistakes, however insignificant and almost forgotten. Even small transgressions are remembered, acknowledged and agreed upon. There are moments when he is at peace with his unhappiness and he understands it. It is apparent and it is clear, and he accepts it as the net result of what he has become. This movie runs a loop in his mind.

***

In the village where he has coffee, is a cat. That cat. That pretty black-and-white cat he first saw as a kitten last spring when he could see. The cat is now pregnant with her own kittens. She looks up at him possibly remembering the time she took protection from him—young and unsure of the world—from under the table where he drank. He gives her solace and a morsel from his plate. The only reason pretty cats survive.

***

After a few hours of not hearing from him, feeling guilty, Amelia has concerns. Was he serious about a last swim? Why, after all these years apart, was she still required to worry about him? They broke because it is impossible to determine where one thing starts and the other stops. In the end, she chose to save herself, and he, realizing the inevitable, chooses to walk away. He wouldn't walk for her through the frozen tundra, like Jack Reid in winter. Both had to stop hurting.

Amelia again tries his cell. It rings on the beach without notice where he left it. The sand, the rocks, the crags need not answer. She calls the Hellenic Coast Guard. "Thanks for calling," they tell her in Greek. "We'll follow up."

Now wisps of wayward and unwanted clouds obscure the sun and the sea becomes colder. But he is made to swim. His rhythm, like it used to be when he was young, so efficient, now syncs within his environment. He has the timing. He is now a swimming machine. Nothing more than automatic movements. Breathe, move, exhale, repeat. But the cold is worrisome. Careful, he reminds. Breath is of air, not sea. Clouds more fully form, like moistened cotton balls. He's tired, but still no worries.

Again, he thinks about Amelia. And now he is cold and tired and thinking about all his past love affairs he has suffered, and it is not warming him, and he is thinking of all the ruined lives he has known. Doing the breaststroke is a good time for final analysis.

Amelia was his first love, and later, after the divorce, Poppie, Greek, the hippy. Kathy, American in the nineties, where he couldn't keep her in enough money. And Lacey—he wouldn't have a child with a moron. And finally, Christina, German, and a culturally unsustainable relationship. And all the in-betweens, the stop-gap relationships, dead from the get-go. Life is both stupid and ridiculous, combined with interesting and funny. Slapstick funny most times. And you increasingly lose people to call when you need to.

Nearby, a dolphin splashes. The bottlenose gives him an exhalation in recognition. Respiration good. Muscles responding as asked. Mental attitude cooperating but much colder now. An impending leg cramp worries. Now he is a boy again when he meets a young girl. Now he knows. It is a Thursday in 1964. He comes to the relationship with the same insistence which has always defined his life. She is girlishly attractive and seventeen. He is hard-bodied and shy and fourteen. She teaches him to swim. Amelia was his first love. He can barely remember what she looked like now. He only remembers the curly, the dimpled, the pink, and the excitement when, every day, they meet. Life can never be as explosive as the day when you discover the new things puberty offers, and a first love. A summer romance. Those two months will always translate to a lifetime. He is so proud to have had her. Amelia destroys him because she can. She destroys him the day she graduates and moves on to college where he remains in high school. He determines to make her his own once again. They marry four years later.

***

After numerous follow-up calls, the Coast Guard discovers his clothing on the beach. He is not wearing a swimsuit. After the hours he is at sea, his body heat might be diminishing.

They unmoor a boat and dispatch a chopper to look for a body.

He is now miles out in open ocean. The destination rock long ago a distant memory. He is becoming hypothermic, is tiring, but will not acknowledge and cannot see. Navigation comes from the direction of the waves.

Now a mental warmth comes over him as he thinks of his mother. She comforts him between her breasts. Everything he will ever need she provides. He has no worries. She guides him, and he is safe. If he dies right now, he will forever live. He is exhausted. His body temperature has dropped. He shivers. Shivering is the body's attempt to warm itself. If he were to talk, his speech would be slurred. His breathing is slow and shallow. His pulse is weak, his body suffers from a lack of coordination, and low energy. Soon he will have a loss of consciousness. He will drown, a type of liquid suffocation. No one will be there for assistance. Breathing will cease.

Now, with every weak stroke and glide, comes a last delirious thought. Saint Seraphim of Sarov wrote, "Swim often and you will feel on earth like the fish in the water." He wishes he could think of something funny in reply. Sick in spirit, for the first time in his life with no clear direction, he does not know how it happened. He used to be funny. With age comes brittleness. He finds himself slipping.

He loses forward momentum, and the dolphin pod discovers him. He floats, almost comatose. They surround him. The pod has received succor from humans before. Conservationists have identified them as a population of bottlenose dolphins living in the area for decades. Lucky for him, they were there. The Coast Guard notices an unusual amount of dolphin swimming around and circulating warming water around the man. It was like a floating carpet of love.

***

Inside intensive care, Amelia asks, "Can I see him?

"We're not allowing visitors," the nurse says. "He's waiting for further treatment."

Now they hear laughter. It is no ordinary laugh. It bellows forth, unceasing, down the corridors of the hospital and startles the other patients. But how can a drowning victim laugh? It is again a Thursday in 1964. His final laugh is in the realization that he could have just as easily drowned, face down at home, in a glass of water, rather than in open sea. Such drama.

Lost Shoe

First published by Balestra Magazine, 4th ed, Aug. 2025

She put her sandy, salt-encrusted foot on the officer's desk.

"That's interesting," Detective McMurry said. "We don't normally see one of those so complete. I'll alert immigration in the capital, Olympia. We'll hold on to that, if you don't mind."

"No, it's mine. I found it. I brought it in so you could document it."

"Yes, very good of you. Thank you for your service," he said in an obligatory tone as he began the report.

Rachel was not from the area. She came from the East Coast after hearing about the bizarre occurrences through the media. She had come in curiosity, and, as she imagined, a documentary scholar. With her second novel finished, she had finally received her divorce judgement. It was now time to explore other avenues. This time, non-fiction. Something about violence and abuse against women in marriage. And to bare her soul. What writers do. To flush out demons.

It had washed up on shore and was buried in the sand. She had returned to look for it again, but nothing. Then, after a week, she found it. There it was, one hundred feet from where she'd seen it first, like it had been waiting for her, expectant, sticking out of the sand like a beacon and a waypoint in the desert.

The morning before, in the hotel of a blood-red dawn, she had opened the twin glass doors to the balcony facing the sea. The flowers were in riot. The air was thick with honey. It was time to witness spring. Grapes were in full leaf, all fruit waited an August harvest.

Trapped between the curtain and the door was a butterfly. Butterflies only have a limited time. She liked butterflies. They struggle to exist. They have a short life. She jostled the curtains, and the butterfly flew free.

She wondered, circumspect, why did she call him that afternoon after finding the foot?

"So, what will we do about it?" Why she continued to use the plural with him escaped her. "So," she corrected, "what will *I* do about it?" It was unusual for her to have contact with him. She was still smarting after a difficult breakup. And why did they break? Because there is no air in space. We cannot breathe water. Butterflies and caterpillars will never talk.

He was surprised at the call. When they first met, her laugh was bubbly. Young, musical, carefree. After the divorce, she found herself forced to leave her newfound independence and apartment in Manhattan. She had traveled to California to pull the trigger on her comatose twin brother in the Haight. It was then when her laugh had become forced, raw, low and without humor.

"Do about what?" He was English, and was typical of his breed—reserved. He set aside emotions and leaned toward misguided loyalty. She was more spontaneous, was given to emotional outbursts. The British. She came to despise him for his coldness and saw him as a self-anointed arbiter of propriety. And someone who attempted to control her.

"You *know* what. Don't be evasive. How can you be so glib about this? It's a shoe…a tennis shoe that—"

"A trainer, you say. Indeed, curious. That's interesting." The British enjoy a good *indeed.* There again was that distant chill. "No doubt the result of a suicide."

"Yes, a tennis shoe, but this one is different. With a foot, for crissakes. With a bone sticking out of it. I know this one has a name and a message. You don't just find a foot washing up on the shore every day. It *could* be a murder. If you come across a turtle on a fencepost, you can bet it wasn't an accident."

"You Americans can be so amusing in your metaphors."

"It seemed to speak to me…" She glanced at her left hand—the finger where the marriage ring is placed, barren now. Her caustic lawyer had said it was the only finger that has a vein directly connected to the heart. The lawyer had shown her teeth. She had baggage with men. Rachel let the thought pass, opting for a more thick-skinned approach—an approach he had schooled her in, one that the Brits excel at, one which she knew he preferred. "Why do you always discount my feelings? I want to do something about it."

"So, someone perished and died in the sea. The harsh marine environment can eat away unexposed skin and bones in no time. You say the shoe is monogrammed? With the initials NW?"

In her research, she found that human feet routinely wash up on the shores of the Salish Sea between Washington State and Vancouver. Modern tennis shoes float, and keep decaying feet in a neat little package, protecting feet from hungry sea creatures. Saltwater preserves.

A writer's synapses are quick to create possibilities. "It was her. I know it was her. What could she have thought about before death? Why do all dying people see the same thing? The dead they had known, attending them, and escorting them to the afterlife." She thought about her twin, piss drunk out of his mind, crushed by alcoholism and his own divorce, smashing his head, falling backward in San Francisco, and the death that came soon after they removed his life support—her decision, as closest kin.

"Hallucinating, perhaps, but the same thing? I think not. And why do you believe the dead are seeing these same things? Are they still alive when they report seeing these epiphanies?"

"It might be cultural. We have a belief that our ancestors are looking down on us. In stressful times, like dying, that is the *first* thing you'd think. Look, death is a process, not a moment, okay? Many who didn't die and came back to life, talk about meeting the deceased."

There was silence between the two. A recent history. "You say the initials NW were written on the shoe?" he repeated, as if he was still interested. "The shoe is pink?"

"A woman's shoe. Yes." As if to document her art, Rachel said, "Here, a woman who did not make it. Here a foot, as if to walk ashore once more."

"An American poet. Brilliant! To be sure, you *are* gifted."

Not knowing why, she told him about the butterfly.

He commented with perfect English dryness, "Without protective lenses, riding a motorbike, a delicate thing such as a butterfly hitting you in the face at speed, can cause much damage." He always thought himself clever. Afterward, he'd stick his tongue into the side of his cheek to signify he'd said something profound, and that others should take note. She could see it through the cellphone. Respect a pundit. In the beginning she thought it charming, continental, but later, pathetic. He still wanted her, she knew. Old chickens make great soup.

***

So, you're sitting naked on that beach off the Pacific Northwest, and a word and a phrase comes to a writer, first as droplets like little unpolished pearls as you watch the undulating sister of the Earth. Waves crash in unending power and hubris, and you think of all the relationships gone awry in the cauldron of your mind and you make note to paper. It is ephemeral, an idea. After, you climb up a craggy path to the only tavern, as simple as a cantina, as elaborate as a hotel, where you go to touch others in social greetings, only to return to that lonely beach, looking for something you cannot ever have or fully describe.

***

When Rachel found the shoe, she quietly sat there, upright in thought, studying it with its femur bone sticking from it, like an unlikely flagpole. It was then she had an internal conversation with it. It seemed to speak directly to her, without sound, in thought. *People said afterwards it was an accidental disappearance. That I slipped overboard. The captain said it in court.* In Rachel's dreamy state, she heard someone, something whisper into her ear. *We were so happy together. Why Robert?*

She could not shake it, and a few days later she confronted Detective McMurry again, "NW? Natalie Wood?"

"New Woman," McMurry said. "A small upstart shoe manufacturer in Columbia. Went under in 2020. The DNA testing pointed toward a Russian ballerina who dramatically committed suicide, jumped from a bridge after hearing she had Parkinson's at age thirty-two. I'm sorry." The officer watched her, wondering if she believed it. It would be months, years before the real story emerged "Another butterfly gone," said the detective about the Russian report. "Of course, this is from the Russians. You know the Ruskies."

Crushed, Rachel checked out of her room soon afterward. Defeated, she had no option other than to believe him. She left without the shoe. She took the coast highway south, to San Francisco, where she would begin her novel about violence and abuse against women in marriage.

A Hat with Attitude

First published by Zest of the Lemmon, Aug. 2025

That hat damned the whole thing. He had bought it in a thrift shop. Inside it said, *Official Indiana Jones.* Ten bucks. A bargain. Almost new, and fedora brown.

Twenty years earlier, in a different direction, younger, he'd traded simple editing work for a vintage leather, black, by Beck's. Of James Dean vintage. With all the zippers and the stars. Short to the waist, heavy-leathered, big-collared, with slant pockets and zippered cuffs. It had a belt with a big silver buckle, and silver stars all over. And it was black as all hell could be. When he wore it, fuck the one who thought he was *Manhattan queer.* But that was when he had been younger, and with another style. He wasn't so tough now, and he had the hat, and like the Beck's leather, the hat made him do strange things.

Before the Beck's, and then the hat, he had been timid and unsure and impotent and sometimes, at night, after a few drinks, foundering, he'd make whelping sounds, of whimpering dogs for their mothers, sounds of longing, sounds of hurt and loss, pain, and emptiness. The sounds of lost love.

He traded the leather after it got him into a barfight he'd lost, for a pair of wedding bands at a hock shop, when an out-of-control librarian agreed to marry. She wore the same librarian clothing every day—cardigans, brown slacks, and loafers. Finished with the musty smells, unleashed, she'd go undomesticated after work. Lamenting the leather when they broke, she said, "Why can't you be stronger? Take charge. Like when we met. I want masculinity, dominance, and romance." He was a blow, a defeat, and a setback in what she'd envisioned—a runaway, unrestricted, after-work life. That was before the hat.

***

Can we examine what we choose to wear, and how it makes us behave? A suit and tie? Bib overalls? Cut-off jeans? A priest's collar? We are what we wear. and what we wear reflects who we want to be.

The hat spoke to him now. He complemented it with a wool coat, double-breasted, brown. The coat and the hat were now. *Thank you hat,* he thought, *for giving me this new identity*. It was again 1930, and the hat liked that.

The hat too large for his head, he wore it cocked, and low when he saw her at the opening. He knew he was being rude when he approached her, but now, NYC direct, fearless and hatted, he went for it like Jones.

The gallery was by the Hudson. She'd been sightseeing with a gender fluid friend from the city, who, annoyed and impatient, waited to collect by the cloakroom.

She had been on her feet all day. A part-time model, detail-oriented, she stopped to examine every artwork. And all the while her feet burned. Stylish women in high heels will kill their feet forever to be taller. Those shoes. Six inches high. Toes crammed and pointed. The coming bunions. At home, in Saigon, where some occasionally still spoke French, she wore Aio Dai, a conservative dress and a conical hat. Elegant and understated. Today she wore city modern, a thigh-high skirt, and low-cut blouse, black. She was shapely, and proud of her legs, her calves pronounced. She became annoyed when men stared.

"You drip sex," he ushered into her ear, even though he thought she might not speak English. She had that exotic look, was younger. There was no mistaking what the hat wanted. "You need a man. Come with me." He took her hand and brought it down low. "Give me your animal sexuality, and you will have everything you came for today." It was the hat talking.

"J'adore ton chapeau," she said with a hint of sarcasm, thinking, *this pig couldn't possibly understand French, anyway.* Didn't he see she was with the one with the close-cropped hair dressed in black workpants? The one without makeup, and sturdy.

"Oui, je suis un gars chic, seulement le meilleur pour vous." He pulled a rabbit from the hat, surprising her. He didn't know he could speak French. *It must be the hat*, he thought. He thought to add a crude French phrase—something about couches and sex—but didn't. At least he had that much sense.

She stole a glimpse at his eyes, hidden under the brim. She couldn't. Overall, he might be attractive, was bold enough, spoke flawless French. And, as men with mental illness had always intrigued her, opening a temporary door, she said to tease, "Impressionnant."

Her eyes were a color which suggested the earliest brown of nature, with eyeshadow of undulating waves of water and things which come in spring. His were of dark *Yin Sanpaku*, with white showing under the irises—a sure sign from nature of insanity, where one's life is threatened by an early and tragic end. He had committed sins against the order of the universe, and he was therefore, under that hat—according to Asian lore—sick, unhappy, insane.

He said, "Come with me and have a drink. I only live a few blocks away." He stopped the hat from talking now. It was his loneliness speaking.

"C'est possibile," she said, teasing, half acquiescing, before a rogue wind, straight off the Hudson, tipped, then yanked the hat off the man's head and deposited it downstream into a frigid river. The woman stood there looking at him openmouthed, with impossible words to describe this fateful and sudden reversal.

She looked at his thin and balding white hair, his miss-shaped skull and his bad teeth and his bulging face, and turning away from him, said, "Soyez bien, au revoir."

He turned and walked the few blocks home. He would miss that hat. The wounded dog would again have his misery.

It seems the brain—like its fickle tenant, the mind—works in strange ways.

A Cold Day at the Beach

First published by Wordrunner eChapbooks,
Issue #2, Micro-prose, Jan. 2025

Stones. Large and small. Stones littered the shore. Most of these stones were from the Paleozoic. Others from pre-Christian marble temple ruins. There was little sand on this beach on the eastern shores of the Aegean. In former times, it was a poor and difficult life in Southern Europe. But now there was tourism. They came for the beaches. And they stayed for the love. Of late, rising off the stones was tough on his old Greek bones.

She came to the beach shortly after he did. She disrobed with little shame or fanfare. She brought no umbrella, only a large towel and a scented tube of sunscreen. She lit a cigarette. Her breasts had always served her well. He watched her lying on her back and apply sunscreen to her breasts, then to her belly, and last to her legs. He was sure he knew her. It was impossible to forget a former lover.

He watched as a cloud and its shadow traveled its way across the beach, changing the colors of the shore, the rock formations, as it passed through.

After some effort in rising, he drifted toward her, trying to act the innocent. He knew it was best to carefully approach a woman on a nude beach. "Excuse me," he said to her as she basked unclothed on the beach. "Are you German Swiss? You look so familiar."

It was October. Tourists were no more. High season was a memory. Only the hardy and the frugal remained. And the lonely on holiday. Every undulating wave exposed a prehistoric rock, looking like a submerged beast or ocean creature.

The sky was baby blue and cotton-balled white. There were no storm clouds, but that could change fast.

"Yes, I am German, born in Switzerland. Do I know you?" She inspected him. He was tanned all over, had a silvery white tail pulled back and hanging down the back of his neck, and sported a hearty Greek mustache. He could not be mistaken for anything else than Greek. He was still fit for his age, as was she, who could still turn heads.

The beach was a cacophony of stone objects. Astronomers have noted that there are more celestial objects in the universe than grains of sand on Earth. How strange that these two souls should meet again.

The alternating clouds and sun, the fresh cool breeze, the crashing surf, all gave notice of fall. Autunm is a brutal time for some, bringing notice of coming winter. They were both middle aged. They were both experienced in the vagaries of love.

"Have you been coming here for a long time?" he asked. He tried to look as attractive as he could. Still wanting her, he went for it. "I think we might have made love to each other one summer, oh, twenty years ago." He smiled a crooked smile—a sly smile which had worked for him before. "You had an English boyfriend at the time, as I remember, a tour guide, working on the other side of the island." How could he put the next as delicate as possible? "You, at times, came to this side to feel unencumbered and free. The Brit was tall.

I don't think he knew we were casual lovers that summer. I met him once. I remember him having the most startling blue eyes."

She looked at him, amused. *Quite the pickup line*, she thought, even if it was true. "Yes, his name is Jonathan. We dated for a while. He followed me to Switzerland, and we married."

"Your name, if I remember correctly, is Sabine."

The German-and-Swiss woman looked out to sea. The ocean always reclaims what is hers. The woman's blue eyes for a moment lost any coldness they might have held and flashed nostalgia for the lost years and the freedom which comes with youth. "Married for some time now," she made clear, sensing he was looking for an opening and an opportunity. She had always been sexually attractive, which both opened and closed doors for her. She thought about her grandfather, who had molested her for years when she had been a young girl. After that, she couldn't stop the boys from coming. "My husband and I have a daughter. She never met her biological father. She has brown eyes, like yours."

She remembered the Greek now. He was shorter than her. He had dark curly hair then and a tight torso. He had been an excellent lover. They were the same age. It had been just pure and simple sexual attraction. A Greek island holiday romance. No strings and no consequences. And certainly, no pregnancies.

She was as bold as he remembered. And as attractive in a more mature way. He stopped smiling. His head turned askew, like a dog who struggled to comprehend. He wasn't prepared for what came next.

"How old is she?" he asked, thinking he was only being polite and following the conversation. "I mean, your daughter."

"She's twenty." There was discrete eye contact now. "Are you here for long? My husband and my daughter are on the other side. I'm sure my daughter would like to meet you. Should we all have dinner together tonight?"

Filter Feeder

Like a gull drawn to a trap, she returned early Sunday morning to the boat at the marina where they both lived. Stuart sat upright in his bunk when her weight swayed the port side. He heard her heavy footsteps on deck. The old boat had worn sails and a tired diesel engine. *Incestuous* moved gently, side by side, tugging at her lines by the bow. Stuart felt the tides changing. It would be low water soon, and he would have to go to work to find another spoil island to farm.

Baby tossed an unopened carton of Marlboros onto her bunk. She opened the lid of the chart table behind Stuart's bunk and placed a small baggie of weed inside for safe keeping. She deposited a small roll of twenties and fifties, held together with a rubber hair tie, into the chart table. "Here, old man, I have the rent. This month's bills are paid," then added with a smirk, "Captain."

"Who, this time?" Stuart wanted to know. She often compared him to Dustin Hoffman in his role as 'Ratso Rizzo.' Not exactly, but close.

"Does it really matter?" Baby asked in evasion. Stuart didn't need to know everything.

"Yes, it matters. We agreed. It matters."

"The guy who works at the marina, in Bluefish."

"The mechanic?"

"No, the skinny kid who pumps gas," she said, ironic, then laughed. "He must have been saving for months."

Stuart was not pleased. It was he who should provide. He knew it was more than the gas pump kid if that was who it was. Dockage and electric were over six hundred dollars this month, and Baby had been gone all night.

One Saturday a month she hung out in her car at the 7-Eleven in Bluefish, the next town over, looking to hook something other than fish. Stuart liked to work. Perhaps today, he thought, he could pry loose some money from somewhere.

"Don't knock it, old man," Baby said, noticing the disdain in Stuart's face. She gathered toiletries and a towel and headed for the shower rooms. "I just covered the bills."

Stuart still owned some tools. At times, he could get work in the nearby boatyard where he could paint a bottom or caulk some seams. Day-help shrimp boats, maybe.

A day before he stopped in to speak with Dick. "The last time I got you some work," the boatyard owner had told him, "It took you so long to finish, the owner lost half the season." The yard boss was muscular, short and thick, and spoke to the point. He wore work clothing daily, even on Sundays, not like his partner—his tall and thin brother, Gerald—who worked in the yard's climate-controlled office all day. Although from the same mother, only one was educated. "So, not this time, sorry."

"Psst. Psst," said Edie, the painter, from under a Chris-Craft. "Hey Ratso, your girl was here yesterday. Spent all the day upstairs, in the boss's office."

Stuart ignored him and kept on walking.

"The boss came out later looking all spent out." Edie laughed. He was always seen under boats. He missed nothing in the boatyard.

Stuart liked to call Baby his daughter. They lived together on the Brackish River, part of the Intracoastal Waterway in South Jersey, an area affected by tides. An Atlantic saltwater inlet, thirty miles downstream, the ocean backed up river water twice a day. At low water it smelled like dead fish. He could count on low tides every day where he could tend to his unlicensed crab traps, harvest dinners of mussels, and dig clams for cash. Hand-to-mouth in a backwater marina in Jersey.

Baby was twenty years younger, uneducated, and still parasitic. She was the daughter of a woman who Stuart had married in a hurry for her meager assets. 'Cupcake' had died in a head-on car crash in Philadelphia the year before. Stuart, asleep in the back, survived. She had been drinking, was going the wrong way. I had been her fault. After he had paid off the mortgage, with whatever money was left, Stuart bought the boat. Baby's principal pursuit was to provide cigarette money for herself. Stuart considered smoking unhealthy and did not approve of the cost. She had a habit of smoking weed, and she relied often on the courtesy and transparent desires of strangers.

Baby, cherubic at twenty, was reasonably good looking, pale white, full-figured and thirty pounds overweight. As a result of a past drug habit, she had bad teeth, which blackened and rotted in her mouth. Her only exercise was cleaning, which she enjoyed, and, in fact, was obsessed with. That was the principal reason Stuart let her stay after he bought the boat. The relationship was one of mutual needs. Friends with benefits now that Cupcake was gone. Baby was not opposed to, and Stuart condoned her turning a trick or two occasionally when the dockage was due—but only if Stuart thought the man was clean and reasonably safe.

One day, Stuart foraged for mussels at a new place at low tide, where an abandoned outcrop of pilings, like a blackened forest of carpenter pencils stood with a story long forgotten at a spillway site, a few miles away. Everyone said it was an abandoned government research site. The WPA dredged the river during the depression so the intracoastal could be a minimum of fourteen feet, and more navigable. They had created small spoil islands along the way with the fill. The islands, barely two feet above river level, were accessible only by water, and he used his small wooden Jon boat. The boat was of wood and constantly leaked. An essential piece of equipment, a cut-out half-gallon container for bailing, floated in the bilge. The mussels which grew on the spoil were exceptionally large. No one ever came to harvest them.

Mussels upon mussels in great clumps of black and iridescent color covered the pilings from the high-water mark to low. He could fill two-gallon containers in minutes, enough for three meals, and enough still grew there to provide many more days of food.

No one bothered with the molluscs on this part of the river. They questioned the purity of the water. Harvesting other shellfish from the muddy river beneath was considered unadvisable.

"Not that again," Baby said that night, turning up her nose. "Let me go out tonight, find some handsome stranger. I'll feed you steak and lobster."

"This is good enough until something better turns up. I'll get some work soon."

Baby made a face and went outside to smoke on deck. "It should have been *you*, old man, in that head-on instead of my mom," she said loud enough for Stuart to hear. "I don't know why you got written in as the beneficiary."

"Because you were a crackhead and a whore, and Cupcake knew it," Stuart shot back. The woman on the powerboat in the slip next, washing her deck, gave Baby a look. Secrets are hard to keep in a marina.

Stuart liked to sauté his shellfish with a bit of garlic and some onions. Leek were better, but more expensive. A tomato gave it color and acidity when he could afford it. After adding lemon, he served it on a bed of spaghetti. A busboy from a local restaurant poured leftover wine from abandoned tables into empty mayo jars and traded it to Baby, who waited behind the eatery, for a few errant feels and an occasional pelvic grind.

It was apparent right away that these mussels were different. The blue-black shells were unusually colored inside, and all had a round and hard accretion. When he investigated further, he determined it was something yellow-colored and stone like, which had to be removed before eating. He tested one between canine and canine. It was soft for a stone and malleable. He knew instantly what it was.

Stuart said he was a writer working on a fiction piece and doing research. "Moluscs are filter feeders," said a professor at a community college nearby. "If true, they would be collecting minerals from the water, or from the leaching of the fill itself."

"Where can I sell gold?" he then asked a friend by phone who lived in another town with internet access. "Who pays the most?" The same day, he rode a borrowed bicycle to a nearby pawn shop jeweler with a few of the miniscule pieces he hadn't already swallowed.

"They're small, smaller than a pebble. I might destroy one in the testing," the jeweler warned, "if that's okay." When he returned from a back room, he said, "Yes, Twenty-Four Karat. Where did you get these?"

Stuart thought better than to answer but did. "My brother in Colorado."

"When you have at least a gram, bring them in and I will cash you out. Being a pawnbroker, by law, in case items are stollen, I have to hold everything that comes in for thirty days. You can get more from a licensed gold dealer, but I pay cash, and up front. *They* pay by check." With a pawnbroker's eye, he knew Stuart did not own a bank account.

"Any idea what each piece is worth?"

"At today's price, by weight, about two dollars. And likely to go up."

Stuart did some quick math. Each trip to the pilings might be worth a hundred dollars or more. It was bank.

"No more outside at night for you, princess. I'm going to be rich," he said dryly to Baby, who previously failed to see any value in mussels. She enjoyed her work. She liked sex. Most sex workers do. When the client looked good, she would have given it up for free, but she liked the money anyway and took it.

For months, Stuart quietly harvested as he always did, and everyone considered this normal. Everyone had to eat in tough times, but soon, the shells piled up under the boat, opened, with the meat untouched. The tides eventually buried or took them away. Everyone walking the dock noticed the accumulation of garbage fish.

Baby showed a few specks of gold to her dealer, and he gave her credit towards future weed. Stuart told a local butcher, and they ate steak on the arm. All the while, the gold stones accumulated in a small, capped pharmaceutical container under the lid of the chart table.

As Baby liked to talk when high, she told the Bluefish gas attendant one day, who told a clammer the next, who told his hairdresser wife, who told everyone.

Word got around. Some watched Stuart. One day the pilings held no more mussels. Not even spores remained to create a new crop. Stuart put a gallon of gas into his outboard and took his skiff up and down the river, but there were no more pilings with no more molluscs on any of the spillway islands.

One day, when the rent was due and Baby was absent, Stuart opened the chart table and grabbed the container of gold, estimating it contained almost ten thousand dollars' worth inside. He replaced the container with one filled with sand, glued the lid shut, and hid the real gold deep inside the boats engine compartment.

A few days later, just before it was time to sell, he discovered the bogus container under the chart table was gone. And so was Baby. She left a note. *"Been good, old man, but time I fix my teeth and show up for a job I got as a cocktail waitress. Tips and tits and tricks. Come to Vegas, old man, I'll fuck you again, for free.* She left the note unsigned except for a smiley face.

Stuart threw the letter into the chart table without ceremony and closed the lid. He could quickly ready the boat. A slip was available in South Carolina. But first, a trip to the pawnshop jeweler was in order. When he got there, he found the container inside the engine compartment was filled with sand.

A Bird, Remorse, A Cane

A version of this story previously published by Culture Cult Magazine, Jan. 2026

In the beginning, the cane had no name. She should have an old-fashioned name. Surely a matronly name, the cane. Like a woman, and capricious in her opinions according to her menstrual cycles. If the cane were Greek, she would be as generous as a woman's hips. As motherly as a woman's breasts. As caring as a woman's heart. But the cane was not from that part of the world, was English, and none of those traits applied.

He was proud of his degree from Columbia University. He carried a framed copy of his degree in ornithology—bird science, and hung it on every wall in every room in his travels.

One day this Greek zoologist happened upon the cane on a visit to London. He wanted steadying and assistance as he walked during his bird watching activities. Not knowing why, he whispered to the cane, "Many species of birds engage in elaborate courtship rituals. Singing, ariel acrobatics, captivating behaviors and displaying bright colors to attract mates. Beauty plays a vital role in sexual attraction." But this ornithologist was not beautiful. He was plain. Sparrow-like. Sparse, beady-eyed, and beakish. A cold and wet bird, seeking solace in any tree available.

He was partial to buying from antique shops. *Dead people's stuff,* he called it. The notice stated that the cane was found beneath a Viking wreck under the Thames. The thick cane was more like a walking stick made of blond, English hardwood. It would be handy through forests, along beaches, or in a dark alley at night if needed. A large silver owl-shaped knob was on top, one you would not want your head to meet on a dark, unprotected night.

He bought it, thinking it would lend him an air of British respectability. He did not need a cane. He was generally fit for his age, except for some unrelated issues. He suffered unsightly feet, a weak bladder, and an impending hearing loss. One eye wandered upon occasion. He became acquainted with the cane after a time. He ignored and would not hear what his acquaintances said about the appendage he admired and eventually could not do without. Those who knew him best said the cane had made him submissive, acting much like an innocent dog might when facing confrontation, lying prone on his back with paws up and pleading, D*on't hurt me, please.*

She soon had a name, the cane. He'd been with the cane now for more than a few years, and with every day that passed, he relied upon her emotionally. He couldn't move without her approval, and he became increasingly more subservient to her. A harsh taskmaster, Magda assumed control. The birder was afraid to be alone and without. He craved companionship and direction. The cane, in time, changed him and changed his personality.

He liked to mimic bird calls. He spoke and they answered.

"Darling, I don't know you anymore," said one bird, a swift, a high-speed acrobat who had known him a long time. "Come back to Greece and become whole again."

"My love, you've changed," said another bird, a swallow, who, never landing, spent most of her days in the air. "I knew you from the old neighborhood, and from the island, but you, from London?"

"Can't put my finger on it, but, yeah, different," said a third bird, a blackbird this time, who specialized in melodious song. "Not sure that cane suits you."

One by one, all relinquished him to the cane. In defense, he tried not to care. She made him strong. He had a companion. He was lonely no longer.

In time, the cane pointed out the many problematic issues in his life. She constantly scolded, "Why can't you be more British?" Underlying everything, the largest question he risked was, "What am I doing with my life here in London at this point? Am I happy living the expatriate life? Is it better living in Greece, on an island, where my friends, the swifts fly in and out in breakneck fashion, and the living is easy?" Was it the proximity and companionship of filial friends, the wrens and the shore birds seen so easily? Or was it better to remain holed-up in a room with the cane?

Underlining all was, could he be happier in any place other than London? As a disaffected American, he had traveled for most of his adult life. He loved to collect passport stamps, never staying long, here or there, mostly a few weeks in birding. In every place he appeared as a visitor and a tourist, commenting always to everyone who would listen about how many places, how many birds in the world he'd known, never really knowing completely any of them.

Certain birds, like crows and ravens, have advanced cognitive skills. Sometimes, the birder wondered whether his bird friends were more adept in responding to changes in environmental habitats than him. He always brought the cane with him because he needed her and her support but always worried about what she could do to him should she want. Such is love. When he became too friendly with beautiful birds, she became ugly.

As with all relationships, after the blazing white of the day comes the rosy hue of sunset, followed by the black of night, until, at the end, the moon takes the stage. Since they were together, he had always spoken to her. After a time, the cane replied, spoke with English arrogance in condemnation, derision and criticism. To her, he was an annoying insect, waiting for the swat. This was no ordinary cane. Whatever she wanted, she could accomplish. And she did so with complete impunity.

And then the cane would pummel him. Sometimes she struck him across his back, leaving welts. She beat him for little reason. Other times there were threats, verbal and psychological accusations, and mental abuse.

One old friend, a wood pigeon in Athens counseled, "You will sleep the night. The morning will come; hurt will pass. Another morning is another hope." He could not part with the cane. The cane was his crutch and his ultimate self-punishment. And at night he dreamed. His dreams were separate from his sleep, and the dreams wouldn't fit into his night. He always woke at 3am, awoke at the insistence of his bladder.

In an attempt at self-renewal, away from the cane, the zoologist lingered one morning on the balcony longing for his friends in Athens, the peregrines. They represented freedom and flight. Now, few of his bird friends were still there for him. He did not see them. He did not sing. They ceased to exist. He stayed at home in London with his crutch. Every evening when in Greece, the swallowtails would fly, breakneck as they do, blitzkreiging a message of hello, and of goodbye, teasing autonomy, emancipation, self-government.

They knew him well. They'd counseled a winged life. Sometimes his eyes wept hard, knowing he could not be a bird, and the tears ran red.

And then the beatings from the cane became unbearable. He was often in trouble with the cane, and the cane was always angry with him. Except for death, sleep is the ultimate escape. But sleep can also produce dreams, and dreams can produce joy. And joy can also keep you alive.

The ornithologist couldn't help but dream about birds. Birds he knew. Birds he wanted to know. Birds he'd previously known. And always dreams about arduous journeys of love. He awoke next to the cane, knowing better but insisting the cane was perfect for his needs and that fate had intervened and had delivered him to her, and that there was good reason for the cane. But fools do not fear until there is no other alternative.

It was that time of year in Greece. A golden blossom at hand, the hint of another change of weather to come. And while it was still mild in the land of Odysseus, the olive trees, laden with purple fruit, gave notice of yellow beginnings on their leaves. They still showed light when the breezes blew their silvery undersides. The other trees, the chestnuts, the persimmons and other fruits gave forth their fruits according to their time. Everywhere leaves tinged with orange, and brown, and green. Should it rain, the pines would come alive and give forth the most refreshing scent. The grapes and the figs, leafless, ghostlike, and withered, waited for resurrection next year in the golden light of autumn.

And all around the earth cried brown, waiting for winter rains to renew. In the lingering light, the dark green color of leaves withered, and browned now of a bush in the pink glow of a setting sun and the steel grey of the sea, the light tan of a barren rock shore, nowhere to go now, the sea a different color. Here, now, before him was complete truth. And he knew he had to act. He eyed the cane resting against the wall, waiting. She would beat him again, knowing what he was about.

When the beating became unbearable, the ornithologist, in a fit, threw the cane, javelin like, into the sea. He was alone once again. Those men marooned on a desert island with only a bird population for sustenance, will soon starve when the birds realize their eggs have no future.

Travels to the Underside of the Known World, Saigon, Part One

A few pages from a journal 2008

Back in 1957 or so, when I was eight, I was fond of talking my mother out of a quarter on a bi-weekly basis. Feeding my addiction to reading, I bought Ballantine and Ace paperbacks. I imagine myself wearing Chinos and a Yankee baseball cap, but I might be romanticizing. I probably wore Keds, and, later, Converse when I was of basketball height. A soda-fountain/stationary store was on Junction Boulevard, right next to Edebohls, the ice cream parlor, which had a revolving wire stand with an assortment of new releases. I bought all my Tarzan series there, as well as other Edgar Rice Boroughs adventure stories. The Pelucidar series were fictional accounts of journeys to a world at the center of the Earth. The Martian series were stories about adventures to another planet. One day I chanced upon a new non-fiction paperback titled *An island to myself.* A New Zealander named Tom Neale, who, after knocking about the Pacific, had made his dreams into reality by marooning himself on a small Pacific coral atoll among the Cook Island Group in 1954. At that time I was five. He was middle-aged. He stayed about three years. At that time, I didn't find it at all strange to identify with someone so much older. Along with the *Swiss Family Robinson,* another tale of the shipwrecked and marooned, I read and reread Tom Neal's book as I was growing up. I suppose this early reading was what prompted me, at thirteen, to get into a fourteen-foot boat with an iffy Mercury outboard and make my own journey from NYC twenty-five nautical miles along the shore of Long Island Sound, to my cousin's house, in Huntington, Long Island. My journeys have apparently not ceased.

At times I wonder about myself. As I approach sixty years old, picking up and creating a new and exciting existence for myself seems so normal now. I feel the only permanent thing in my life is the concept of impermanence. This reinventing seems to take place at six-to-eight-year intervals. I had never been to Southeast Asia. After an aborted six years in America as a licensed Realtor—certainly an experiment using a defective hypothesis, whether inductive or deductive I can't tell—I never thought I would be in a third-world metropolis dressing professionally in fine business attire and shaving every day, enjoying the respect of the local folk and trying to understand Asian morality. Never would I have thought that I would have such enormous satisfaction in teaching and knowing that every one of my students would carry something of me into the rest of their lives. Teaching is much like being a parent. You worry about your children and want for them the best.

I've been here in Saigon for just over seven months. From the airport, the taxi deposited me in the central district. Life has settled to the point that soon it might be time to sever the cord between me and the *Backpacker* district in the center where I live to a more ethnic neighborhood in HCMC. I mean, it's okay here; I have all the amenities I need at my doorstep within walking distance, restaurants, bookstores, drinking places, but there's too many goddamned tourists crawling about. White-skinned gawking giants in Liliputia. The scene here is very similar to the West Village in NYC. A must-see when in town. I find myself trying to avoid other foreign teachers when I see them as well. They come here to eat and drink in my neighborhood where everybody speaks English. Except for the teachers who I'm forced to interact with at work, the only contact I have with other human beings are my Vietnamese friends.

I suppose I have always been something of a loner. My students see me as something of an odd-ball—an old fish in a young pond.

For the past seven months, I have taken certain responsibilities to support the constant hordes of street vendors selling everything from fake leather faux Gucci wallets to small doses of Tiger Balm and knock-off designer sunglasses. If I can't force myself to buy, I at least try to give a little of the local money and always give smiling support. They all know me. We know each other by name. We see each other every day. I have many friends in the street people. I do this because I was a *Street Freak* myself in Berkeley, way back in 1969. I panhandled—excuse me, ahem—for the free clinic to support myself, and I have to say that, in many ways, I am still a *Freak*.

The locals constantly invite me to Vietnamese parties, weddings, and dinners at their homes, where I try to avoid eating and politely decline dog. Although I feel like I know many people here, I get the sense that many more people know me. It is a constant balancing act to maintain an even yin-yang proportion between work, finances, and relationships.

Since my early Job Corps days more than twenty years ago, I have loved teaching. My students like me very much. It takes me varying amounts of time, but once I get my class on my wavelength, *they're mine.* I can see it in their eyes—the rapture, in the attention that they give—and they hang on my every word. They listen *to* me, not *at* me. I enjoy excellent feedback from them, as well as the school administration. My salary is enough to maintain a decent standard of living, as well as stashing away some money if my circumstances change. I have traveled within Vietnam and last February, visited Cambodia.

Cambodia is, shall we say, the wild west of SE Asia. As of this writing, Pnom Penh, the capital, is raw, decadent, filthy, and a real shithole. It is a vile city, complete with rampant prostitution, drugs, and guns, all out there, accepted, and in plain view. It wasn't five minutes upon my arrival when a hooker approached me, wanting entrance to my room. That would never happen in Saigon. There, you have to strategically place yourself in a discreet location and wait for someone who actually would like to meet and spend time with you. Culturally and economically, Cambodia is Thirty to Forty years behind Saigon. And there is a reason for that.

The Americans invaded Cambodia during their aggression in Vietnam, hoping to use it as a staging ground for their war against the North Vietnamese. Location, location, location. They bombed whole rural villages out of existence, and everybody who remained, fled to Pnom Penh. When the Americans finally realized they couldn't win against a tenacious Vietnamese who had been repelling various invaders for hundreds of years, they left an enormous void in Cambodia, which the Khymer Rouge were only too happy to fill. Enter the Maoist Khymers. The Khymer Rouge immediately set to put right Cambodian philosophy. They separated Pnom Penh into four-quarters, N E S &W, and put a different military governor in those four places. They rounded everybody up one day, and either chased them into the surrounding countryside—if they were lucky—or herded them into one place to execute them. The Khymer Rouge, being puppets of the Red Chinese, had a particular hatred for the bourgeoisie. They thought that everyone should be farming to provide for the collective, not enjoying the fruits of capitalism. Depending on where you were that day, you wound up either dead or running in one of four directions. The Khymer Rouge separated entire families that day, N E S &W. Later, on one subsequent day, they slaughtered nine thousand people in the killing fields outside of Pnom Penh. The site is now a tourist attraction run by a Japanese concern, and visitors can pay two dollars to see all the skulls on display.

Vietnam invaded Cambodia in the late 1970s, liberated the Kyhmer people, and took a large part of the Mekong Delta as recompense. Today, many charities work in the country to prop up the economy, and if it were not for the NGOs, Cambodia would be in even worse shape.

I spent about four days in the sleazy *Backpacker's* area, which featured windowless rooms, maybe a fan, constructed on rickety wooden platforms built onto the lake, and a hole in the floor in lieu of a toilet. There was no hot water. Budget to be sure, five bucks, great polluted sunsets. Word on the street was that the whole lake was to be filled and the neighborhood razed. I needed to cleanse myself. I made it to Sihanoukville, on the Cambodian coast, on the Gulf of Thailand.

The entire area of Sihanoukville, where fat white Western tourists line the beaches in a region billed as The Cambodian Costa Del Sol, was popular by well-to-do Pnom-Penhers before the Khymer Rouge. The Maoists burned the place to the ground, and it is just now coming back, but the hulking ruins of what used to be villas are still visible. Be careful in the jungles not to step upon unexploded landmines. Russians have a special place here, and the men avail themselves frequently of the inexpensive women. Western tourists loll around the beaches to get their daily dollar oil rubdowns by dark-skinned Khymer women—a product of a caste system which kept most of the people entrapped in a life under the sun. The people here have almost a Mongolian look. The Cambodians hail from wandering Indian tribes. They smile a lot and will do anything for a dollar to include selling their children and their own souls. Buddhist monks pose for pictures with tourist women in two-piece bathing suits. I got the distinct impression that the young guesthouse owner would have shared his wife with me for a price. The NGOs supply the ruling elite with brand new Range Rovers and Mercedes, hoping that this new prosperity will filter down to the masses, but, so far, tourism, along with the inherent pitfalls, is the only way to a better life. I was astounded one day at the beach, when young children vendors, shouted the F-word interspersed in every sentence.

At the time of this writing, Cambodia is relatively new to tourism. Western tourists can still get over on the locals, but this will change as Cambodians will ultimately learn to flip the switch and take advantage of tourist needs and target their seemingly bountiful wallets. English levels are low. Few English language schools exist away from the capital city. Larger resorts are built around gambling casinos, something non-existent in Vietnam. Compared to Pnom Penh, Saigon is a sophisticated place. Comparing Saigon to any city in the West is apples and oranges. After about ten days in Cambodia, my holiday was over and I was more than ready to return to Saigon, where the Vietnamese take pride in incessant cleaning, quite a contrast to the Cambodians who will throw trash around and pretend not to see it. The

Vietnamese remind me of an obsessive girlfriend I had once—always cleaning. As soon as you cross the Cambodian border into Vietnam, the whole scene changes. People are dressed well, have motorbikes. There are signs of healthy commerce and an infinitely better lifestyle. Violent crime does not exist in Vietnam. Here, if someone steals something from you, you're stupid and inattentive. In Cambodia you see mini-vans stuffed with people, cargo strapped to the tailgates, six people riding on top, and oxen crossing the highway in nonchalance.

More words about my life teaching here in Saigon. As I've said before, teachers are held in high regard in Vietnam, and there is plenty of work for a good teacher. Standards are tightening though, and pretty soon, the traveling backpacker who just happens to be a native English speaker won't be able to teach and get his ten-dollars-per-hour beer-money. As of this account, a good teacher with experience and credentials gets twenty. Lately we're seeing, along with hordes of unemployed expats leaving their own English-speaking countries for lack of work—teachers coming from Korea, where I've heard students are lazy, bored and with an attitude, and China, where there are fly-by-night schools, where sometimes it is difficult to get paid. Chinese language schools will take anybody, and there is a huge call for teachers, but still they come here. No doubt the word is out that Vietnam is a great teaching destination. The students are serious about learning, and most of the schools are run in a professional manner.

I've been meaning to say something of the concept of personal space here in this crowded part of the world. Lots of people are in a limited amount of space. You can see it everywhere. On the street walking. In the motorbike madness at high speeds. Indoors and out. Everyone is aware of the space they take up and try to be considerate of the space that others in their same universe need. You have to move around people here. You can't occupy the same space at the same time. Doing so would cause a crash, an accident, an unfortunate scene. Often you are compelled to walk in the street, because the Vietnamese use every available sidewalk space to sell their wares. You have to move around others to negotiate your way toward your intended destination. The cars and motorbikes, who also have the right to their space have to be aware of you walking, and they steer around you. This makes someone else with those same rights walking or driving in the opposite direction change course to compensate. It all makes for an unbelievable dance—a ballet if you will—all to some music inherent in the place. Tourists disrupt this rhythm, insisting upon the music of their own country, they often move along, oblivious of any apparent local social grace. Tourist thugs. It took me a week to hear the music and to join the dance. When I got on a motorbike, I realized the rule. If you can see it coming and it is in front of you, it is your responsibility to allow for another's right to available space. It's a lot like speeding down a very crowded sidewalk at rush hour, in New York. Only at higher speed.

Right now, we are entering the rainy season, where short bursts of pelting rain knock the flowers off bushes and forces the locals to seek momentary indoor shelter. All commerce stops. I came here at the tail end of monsoon season, and, frankly, I agree with the locals. It's better to have an afternoon of rain to clean and to wash the streets and to cool things down. Far better than the six months of dry incessant heat where the temperature rarely goes below Ninety-Five degrees and often breaks the triple-digit mark. I try to arrange a short drive to school, as more than once I have ridden my motorbike through knee-deep flooding in my fine business attire and Italian lace-up shoes.

Being an odd-ball teacher, I make my classes fun. My current school allows me complete academic freedom if I stick to the teaching points. Classes are two hours long with a fifteen-minute break. In the first portion, I teach pretty much from the book, introducing liberal amounts of conversation. The second part is all mine, where I concentrate on intonation, stress, pronunciation, and vocabulary. It is amazing how many classroom activities I've collected in the seven months of teaching again. If nothing else, my classes are interesting and fun. We laugh a lot too. All the time.

I have weekday classes for young adults in the upper levels. Two mornings a week, I teach college preparatory classes. On weekend mornings, I teach children. I have Tuesdays off. I'm teaching about twenty-five hours a week, enough when added to about ten or so hours of unpaid classroom prep. I could teach more, but find that when I do, quality goes down. I need to be fresh and energetic in the classroom, never tired or boring. My students appreciate it. I get plenty of teacher support—something I did not feel at the last school where I taught.

But change is in the wind. The school is going through some sort of identity crisis. The ESL field has plenty of competition here, but I don't think they can compete with the more glitzy schools which seem to be gaining a larger foothold on the emerging market of students here in Vietnam. Other foreign language schools have contacted me, and have two resumes out there. Most likely I will soon be working at another school soon which offers better money and school facilities. For now, I have a contract until

December with my present school, and I will have to give them priority.

When I left the States this time around, I took nothing but a backpack. My one backpack has now developed into two. I've bought clothing for work, some DVDs and a few books. Before leaving the States, I sold my entire collection of books of more than five hundred volumes. I resolved never to return to the states. Ex-pat. The guy who bought the bulk of my books called them *eclectic.* I had maintained this personal library for more than fifty years. He'd never seen such a mass of nautical related material. The conscious decision when leaving was that I would *not* do the same thing as I did when I left for Europe, by putting everything in storage. Absurd. For eight years I paid monthly to keep those ridiculous possessions, all of which I could replace. If you have to worry about it, it just ain't worth having. Pretty soon, your possessions wind up possessing you. For my journey, I brought shoes for work, a pair or two of dress pants for work, shorts, and T-shirts, some writing materials, my laptop, and a few books I had kept after selling my library. At the last moment, after finding a small space left in my pack—I don't know why I did it, I stuffed Tom Neal's book—*An Island To Myself.* It's dog-eared, yellowing, and falling apart, but I just reread it after buying it better than fifty years ago. It explains a lot.

Travels to the Underside of the Known World, Part Two

A few pages from a journal 2011

A long time ago, in 1958 when I was seven or eight, my parents began to ship me off to camp Pratt for a few summers, somewhere in the country, up in the mountains. I don't remember where—most likely Pennsylvania. It was just two or three weeks away from home. Camp counselors suggested we all come up with a nickname. I chose Homer. Perhaps subconsciously I chose that name because I was proud of being Greek, I seem to remember thinking it had an old-timey country ring to it, but everyone at camp thought it was because I was good at baseball. I really can't say why I picked that name, but deep down I think it was the former reason. In essence, all Greeks are philosophers. Some are poets.

I learned to swim there. I was seven or eight. Up until then, my only experience with water was salted. It floats you well. Lake water swimming was more of a challenge. I remember struggling to stay afloat, the only requirement for swimmer status, and I was very proud to be proclaimed at the end of that summer, as a *swimmer*. My swimming continues.

What possesses people to jump into lion cages? I have read about someone found dead, mauled in a big cat enclosure at a zoo. I read about it when I taught English in Nuremburg, Germany, where they have a very lifelike zoo. Tiergarten, I think it was called. Someone had entered under the cover of darkness and approached the lion. The lion, surprised by the human's lack of authority and pluck displayed by the zookeepers, at first didn't know what to do. Being bred in captivity, the lion attempted an exploratory cuff across the face, and smelling blood, reverted to instincts. Had someone placed the human there as food? What had gone through the human's mind at that last moment? The lion had to be destroyed. It could never be trusted with humans again.

A few weeks ago, I marked the beginning of my third year in Saigon. Milestones, a sense of accomplishment, and cause for further reflection are somehow in order at describing my feelings at this point. The tail end of my stint in Germany, with a failed attempt at marriage and a lost family, followed by an aborted six-year attempt in Florida as a licensed Realtor, had me feeling, shall we say, a bit psychotic. It was the market crash in 2008. When I left America this last time, I thought I would never return. When I got off the plane in Saigon, I knew I was where I wanted to be. But to be fair, life is like a train. We all have to pay for our passage.

During the first six months or so in HCMC, I succumbed to the strangest maladies. Apart from the so-called Tourist Flu, which everyone gets after the first week in a faraway place, I had frequent colds, blotches on my face, respiratory illnesses, facial twitches, and peeling skin on my fingers and toes intermittently for the first few months. You can get antibiotics in any pharmacy here without a prescription.

All is gone now. Thankfully I have acclimated, except for occasional bouts of coughing which I get from working with children on weekends. I still smoke, but I am confident that the tar and nicotine coating my lungs protects me from the Saigon air. Culturally, I adjusted very quickly—a tribute to my New York City upbringing. I have had three different motorbikes—the first one stolen—and about five or six short time affairs with twentysomething girls—bad girls—and now, a full-time girlfriend. A 'good girl.' She is thirty-two years old, recently divorced, and with a two-year-old son. I am her second lover.

Oh yes, after a year in the tourist sector, I am now ensconced in a more glitzy neighborhood, still in the center of Saigon. My circumstances have markedly improved. I have joined the ranks of the bourgeoisie and live in an apartment, with too many rooms sheathed in black marble on the highest floor of a large building, far above the pollution level.

A note on the subservience of women in this part of the world—much like Greek women, the Vietnamese are trained from early girlhood to take care of and to dote upon their men like a mother would. It is their responsibility to take care of the domestic needs of their mates, to do the cleaning, the shopping, the cooking, as well as any other needs a man might have in the conjugal bed. Most men here couldn't explain how to boil water. Two types of women are here. The ones who save themselves for marriage and the ones who will love you for a price. Faced with this undying devotion, the Viet men I know, by contrast, are *dogs*. It's completely understandable as you are unable to walk the streets without being assaulted by the raw sexuality of the women. Many of them dress attractively. Even the older, poorer women have an underlying aura about them. They walk about in this warm climate in these very thin cotton pajama-like things. Others, if they can afford, get themselves decked out, like Japanese hookers, in tight-tight designer jeans, low at the hip, revealing cleavage and asscracks, and showing fancy brassieres at every opportunity. And oh, spiked heels.

Up until seventy years ago, most Viet women went topless, until the Catholic missionaries put a stop to that. Most Vietnamese men cheat on their wives. When their wives find out, and they eventually do, it ends in divorce. Here, it takes four weeks. Usually, the tip-off is a marked reduction in the available money left in the checking account at the end of the month or the unwise practice of not erasing all telltale cellphone messages common throughout the known world. The woman, free now of moral constraints, can do what she likes. In private.

Here, you cannot hold hands in public or touch each other, as is common in the West, or kiss, or do anything else that would cast an unfavorable light upon the woman. It's called saving face. Behind closed doors, however, look out. As in all repressed societies, pent-up frustrations lead to an explosion when the lights are out.

So, it's been over two years now. Almost three. I have been working every day since I arrived. Comparatively, I make about twenty times what an educated local worker earns. I've been saving money, even in these economically pressed times. Hordes of foreign teachers here now. Some have come from China, disillusioned by the quality of schools there. Some have come from Korea, disgusted with the spoiled students there. Some have come from Indonesia, where the government got fed up with the low quality of teachers and tossed them out. But most have come because they were unable to find work in their respective fields, in their own English-speaking countries. You can tell by looking at them that they are grumpy, scowling, unable to make the cultural leap between their own country and where they are now. Frankly, I wish they would go home. This is the only thing I do not like about living here.

I should say something of this burning fetish that the Vietnamese have. It seems to go along with ancestor worship, belief in ghosts, and the afterlife. When I first arrived, I noticed people burning paper in small metal pots, outside their homes and stores, which are most frequently one and the same. I thought they were just burning household garbage. The other day, while walking along a busy street corner, I happened across a small group of people—family of the deceased I presumed—burning a 3D cardboard effigy of a generic motorbike. The group had heads bowed in respect. No doubt the scene of a horrible motorbike accident of which in this city, are many. Or maybe they were praying for a shiny new motorcycle, I don't know. I didn't ask. Another day, while sitting in a street-side beer joint, one of the waiters took the time to honor his deceased by lighting something of a paper bonfire right next to the ass-end of a delivery truck which was unloading. I took solace in that it was probably diesel-fueled and not that volatile. The Vietnamese believe that fire purifies and that smoke brings spirits to the heavens. From my restaurant table, I have witnessed foreigners enter, sit, browse the menu, then leave without order or comment. Inevitably, a waiter will light up a few pages of newspaper, swish it over, around, and under the insulted table, then cleanse the trail of the would-be foreign guests. They do find this a very funny thing to do. Other foreigners seated in the restaurant stare at them in disbelief.

I would like to say something about the Viet-Kieu—that is, the South Vietnamese nationals who were airlifted from Vietnam after the fall of Saigon in 1975. Many of them are returning after thirty years of exile in the states. I have a lot of English-speaking Viet friends here who were American collaborators during the war. The lucky ones were assisted out by the Americans. The others were all herded into *re-education* camps North, around Hanoi. Some languished there for years until they convinced the Communists of their past errors in thinking.

The Viet-Keiu relocated to places like New York, Texas, Florida, Minnesota, and San Franscisco, to build families. They became American citizens and are damn proud of it. They are just now returning, due to a relaxed feeling in Hanoi, and from a desire in that government to join the international community. Without exception, the Vietnamese want to know if I served in the US Army at that time and what I am doing in Saigon now. When I tell them that I was a Peacenik and that I don't believe in war, they are perplexed. When I tell them that I came here *not* from guilt but of an embarrassment over what America did back then, they are surprised. When I ask them what the purpose was for all those years of killing and point to the resultant ruling government in Hanoi, they fall silent. As I've said before, an enormous chasm in thinking still exists between Saigon in the South and Hanoi in the North. The Viet-Kieu still don't trust the government in Hanoi and still look over their shoulders when they come here.

I come across many ex-GI's returning, looking for closure. It is a good thing, and I wish more would come to put right the guilt left over from the US aggression in Vietnam. Most do not fault me for abstaining.

I now live in a more ethnic neighborhood in the Central District. By *ethnic*, I mean there are Vietnamese, Chinese, Thais, Cambodians, and people from Laos. Makes for a colorful neighborhood. I get to see very few Western tourists. Just fine by me. After spending years in the tourist area, I much prefer looking at Asian faces. Who I *don't* get to see on a daily basis are the French, who are arrogant, demanding, lingua-phobic toward anything other than French, and horrible restaurant patrons. They refuse to leave a tip. And, after one hundred years of French domination here, they still think they own the place. Likewise, I am happy to say that Aussies, who act even more stupidly on holiday than Americans, have ceased to cross my vision and path. In fact, the Australian teachers who I know here can't even speak English. At least as I know the language. Foreign teachers—the bane of living in a developing country. Wannabe Expats here only for the money, or the beer or the women. They, normally, are pasty-faced blue-eyed fresh college grads unable to get a job in their own country. Too, the occasional Swede, who wonders why he has lost all his money that he thought he had safely ensconced in his shirt pocket, along with his return flight ticket. Gone after a Twenty-Four-Hour drinking binge. Astonishing, one guy lost a thousand dollars, right from his upper shirt.

Some snapshots and vignettes:

Most Viets will do anything to speak to a foreigner in English, if it is for free. I try my best, but it becomes annoying at times, due to this is what I do daily with my students. Sometimes I just want to relax.

Heavy-duty three-wheeled loud smoking motorbikes for hauling construction materials. Usually, the operator has his girthy wife along to help him push-start the thing.

Men urinating against a lamppost with impunity. I twice saw a homeless person squat over a sewer in full daylight and take a crap. But really, I saw that in Paris once near the Louvre; only, it was a woman and there and a bush was handy.

Four people traveling on a small motorbike. Sometimes I see five, but the fifth is always an infant and riding between the operator's legs. Motorbike accidents occur daily. You can always tell if someone has died, the police outline in chalk the deceased on the pavement.

Ethnic Viet women from the countryside coming to Saigon to make a few dollars a month to send back to their rice-farming families. They ride bicycles, and wear conical hats and sport pajama like cotton outfits, loose and airy. Zooming around the city like fairy apparitions, they are incredibly alluring.

One more word about the concept of *Face*. The Vietnamese will do anything to avoid admitting that they made a mistake, for to do so would lead to the embarrassment of losing face. For those who know the concept of the Greek *Choryo,* this sprawling city of almost nine million is like one big Greek village. Everyone looks, everyone watches, everyone talks. Those that make the unfortunate mistake of doing something that would cause their family shame, get shunned. Old-fashioned thinking, yes, but it does tend to keep behavior appropriate at accepted levels. Many of my girlfriend's family did not speak to her when, a month before her divorce, they discovered her boyfriend was a foreigner. We were unwise enough to let people see. They did not confront me. She received open sneers.

So, three years on here in Saigon, I can say that I am still happy. I am working, relatively healthy, and in love. What more? I don't know about hitting a *Homer* with my life, but it can be said I am more than content than I have been for a long time, at least for the moment. Even when sailing around in Greece—although I loved the lifestyle—I had my bad moments. Some scholars depict Homer as a wandering minstrel who walked as far as Chalkis to sing at the funeral games of Amphidamas. What we have here is the image of a blind, begging singer who hangs around with little people: shoemakers, fisherman, potters, sailors and elderly men in the gathering places of harbor towns. So, I continue my voyage.

Zephyrhills

Newspapers, print-outs, news clippings and coffee cups cover all desks in the room. The receptionists man the telephones up front. Throughout the building, the station broadcasts live.

"Where did you find that? I didn't see it," Biondi says.

Hanny Persius and Sebastian Biondi sit in the newsroom reading the Sunday edition of the *St Pete Times.* Degan, the station manager, is absent. Biondi's feet are up on his desk. Hanny does not have a desk, he is just past probation, he uses a communal table outside of the newsroom.

"Page three, second column. It's a short blurb, a notice about how the Zephyrhills City Council will meet to discuss reversing their recent renaming of Sixth Street to Martin Luther King Boulevard. Apparently, the motion to be considered is to re-name it back to Sixth Avenue. I think I might head that way Tuesday night," Hanny says. "Might be some fireworks. Never heard of that happening before. Have you?"

"Nope, never have. Yeah. Okay, sounds good. You got three minutes for the story. No more." Biondi says.

Hanny knows he can stretch it if it is good. He always does.

"Here, I got some background." Biondi is already on Wikipedia. "The city of Zephyrhills, thirty miles from

Tampa, was incorporated in 1914…*blah, blah, blah*." Biondi scrolls down, "In 1941, the city had a sundown policy forbidding Blacks from living within the city limits."

"Wouldn't ya know it?" Hanny says. "Racism in the South. The city has a population of just under twelve thousand, of which, under six hundred are Black."

"Just another white-bread Pasco County Florida city," Sebastion Biondi, WKKE's Black news anchor says. Some say he is a DEI hire. Most hip cats at the station call him *The Voice*. "Come back with a good story."

Tuesday afternoon, Hanny packs his gear and heads north to the meeting, scheduled for 7:30pm. He wants to set up his sound early and to get some comments from those just arriving.

Outside, a young man, hands out information to Whites walking in. Chris Tomacello—a twenty-something resident of Zephyrhills who heard about the meeting on National Alliance's website, distributes the hate group's message to other attending Whites. His voice sounds like a cracking adolescent. Hanny presses the record button and points a mic.

Tomacello says on tape, "I, I'm a White separatist, and I believe in the separation of the, uh, the different races," Chris Tomacello feels the importance of being interviewed. "All the Jewish influences, all the Blacks, all the race mixing and stuff—I'm just completely against it all, and, uh, as to naming the street after Martin Luther King, it's not ethical, or logical." Chris hands Hanny a brochure, with swastikas and men in white hoods and others, heiling Nazi salutes.

Zephyrhills City Hall is a simple affair, just a block building with plaster walls, fluorescent lighting, and ceiling fans. In time, it jams with participants. People sit on folding chairs wherever they can, while others stand against walls.

Hanny goes to the speaker's podium and tapes his mic, which has a small white box attached which reads, WKKE to the adjustable one provided by the city for the PA system. It is better to get sound direct from the person speaking rather than rely on secondhand sound taken off the room's PA system. Some venues have an amp which reporters can tap into, this one does not. Hanny does a quick scan. There are no other news outlets in the room. *Oh, yeah,* he thinks, *breaking story.*

The City Commissioners sit in upholstered chairs at a long table against a far wall, where one seat is empty. The meeting is about to start. Making a statement entrance, a petite, well-built blonde enters, wearing a red dress and bringing with her a confident step. Hanny is interested. The meeting is called to order. After discussing city business of various sorts, they introduce the topic of Sixth Avenue. It is what most have come for. The podium is open for comments.

***

This, from Sebastian Biondi's live intro, written for him by Hanny, at the beginning of Hanny's report on Wednesday, 27 April 2004. Biondi's deep resinous voice takes to the waves. "The City of Zephyrhills has voted three times on the name of one street. Sixth Avenue for a short time was known as Martin Luther King Jr Boulevard. White residents who live on the street selected a woman, Gina White, to the city council after she promised to petition the council to revert to the original street name. WKKE's Hanny Persius has the story."

***

When Hanny returns to the station, even though it is late, he processes sound. The next day, he scripts the story and lays it down on tape. "Now you see it, now you don't," Hanny begins the report. "Last night, the Zephyrhills City Council voted three-to-two, effectively removing Martin Luther King's name from street signs on the former Sixth Avenue. Most Council members caved into angry White voters, who made their wishes clear ten days ago by electing Gina White, a political neophyte, whose only platform was the name change. Tensions ran high as White residents insisted the numerical grid system of streets were better than the name Martin Luther King Jr. Gina White, a platinum blonde in a red dress and red spike heels, the newest member of the Zephyrhills City Council." Roll Tape:

***

During the evening of the hearing, Hanny holds his Sennheiser in one hand, his recorder in the other.

Gina stands from her chair so Hanny can get a good look—her face, her body, her legs, the shoes. Gina responds to Hanny's first question, her voice measured, soft, and velvety.

She says, "It has nothing to do with what the street name was changed to. It has everything to do with the fact that the residents and property owners of Sixth Avenue had no voice in whether they approved of the street name change—or not."

Hanny hits her with a quick scenario, "But, don't you think a lot of people don't like the fact that the city counsel changed the name of the street to the name of a slain black civil rights leader?" Exasperation is in his voice. Gina has a way of speaking, seducing, like she is talking lovelies into your ear, intimate, and Hanny right now is her intended.

"Perhaps," Gina coos. "During my campaign I talked to almost every single resident on Sixth Avenue, and out of all the people I spoke to, only two people, that were White, mentioned to me that they were flat-out racists. But, uh…" She goes for the throat. "I certainly experienced more racist attitudes from the Black community than I have from the White members of the community."

Hanny assesses. Gina strikes him as a pretty little girl, precocious, wearing mom's sexy grown-up clothing, trying to make a splash in an increasingly grown-up world. She is turned on by the mic pointed inches from her face, and Hanny wonders what it would be like to fuck a pushy, outspoken conservative. But, oh, that short red dress. Fish-belly white.

The podium is open to comment. From Hanny's report: "Tom Callins, a resident of Zephyrhills and a Vietnam vet, linked Martin Luther King to un-American activities." Most days he wears camo fatigues, black Army boots, and an Army cap. "To me," Callins begins, "it is a contentious issue, because Dr. Martin Luther King, as an anti-Vietnam person, ranked right up there with John Kerry, and Jane Fonda, in that he did not support American troops who were living and fighting a war and dying, and he belongs right there with them. And I can tell you that thousands of Vietnam vets would agree with me."

And Hanny has it on tape. The wounds of war and an ungracious homecoming rode heavy on this man. A pacifist, Hanny chose not to participate in the conflict, and certainly did not spit disrespectfully on those returning at the time.

At the podium, a heavy-set Black woman in her sixties, who lives on Sixth Avenue, does not want to be identified, becomes emotional in her appeal to keep the MLK name. Her hands shake as she speaks in a start-stop manner, the intensity of sentiment hard to control, and she says in a loud, bold voice, "What I wanna say, is that—I want my mother to stand up." The woman's mother rises from the audience, greyed, passive, broken, spiritless.

"And for no other reason you don't let that name change stand, you do it for no other reason, you do it for this lady, who worked..." The words come quickly in her head. She has difficulty getting them out. "That was *cruisin'* land," she gybes. "And this here woman worked for ten cents an hour, while we were runnin' around—" she sniffs, about to cry, and her voice breaks—"hungry and tired, so that *you people*—" her voice under control now—"that don't understand, that we are a community, can live in your fine houses and drive your fine cars, and do everything you can—not just me as a Black woman but to the poor White people of this community. So just for *her*—she worked day and night. And when she was sick and couldn't get up and work? They made her work anyway." Her voice strengthens and grows louder. "I'm not livin' in the past," her voice and manner have moral decency now. "I'm living today, because my mother's here right with me. And anyone here, that can tell me that you worked for ten cents an hour and raised four *fine* children," she finishes flat, "you do that." She leaves the podium and sits next to her mother, and Hanny gets it on tape. Applause erupts from the audience.

Gary Winston, a Black Teacher wearing a brown suit jacket and tie, wearing brown pressed slacks, attempts to educate the city council on the MLK legacy. He speaks in a quiet, measured tone. "History will judge the actions that each one of us takes. The true nature of tonight's events are met by the same re-interpretations of laws that have been so effectively used to shackle free people of this country. What makes Martin Luther King worthy of honor has everything to do with what makes America great. Freedom for all men. Martin Luther King's legacy should transcend this debate. Let the sign stand, as we recognize what real freedom means to *all* of its citizens. Thank you."

Every White face on the council, except Gina's, point eyes downward. Gina looks like she is ready to rebuke but holds her tongue. She looks toward Hanny, who loves every soundbite.

Richard Dayton of Zephyrhills, who can't believe that it is all about a name, approaches the podium. He relives a Dade City riot years ago. He speaks in an accusatory tone, with a southern Black accent. "They treated us like we were slaves. They beated us with handcuffs. They sprayed us with water hose. They beated us with biff clubs—None of you all know that." He looks everyone on the council in the eye. "They had dogs, canine dogs at us. None of you all know that." His voice softens. "And we speakin' on, an' you goin' argue on a name. A name. A name that means something, to *us*." Hanny has it. The audience applauds. The man is done. The council give a blank look. They wait for the next speaker.

From Hanny's report: "The Reverend J. Blackburn, of the Zephyrhills Church of God, reminded the council of Dr. King's Hand-in-hand philosophy and brought up some old skeletons. He spoke as if from the pulpit."

"Ya know?" the reverend confronts, "it's a shame."

Six White faces on the council stare back uncomfortably. Gina, the seventh, looks amused.

The reverend J. Blackburn continues. "And ya know? I'm ashame of ya. This is a city since I grew up, a city that I loved. First ya didn't want us to go to your schools. Even the principal as I remember, said, before any Black or any niggas came into his school, that he would close the doors, or he would quit. What kind of community *is* this?"

Again applause.

The Reverend quotes from a Bible verse then returns to his seat.

***

Hanny tries to be judicious when editing soundbites. There is a lot of good sound. Biondi said three minutes. Hanny knows it will be more.

Again, from Hanny's report: "Zephyrhills City Manager Stanley Medina, who spoke last, was the only White person at the meeting who spoke for Civil Rights. He asked the council to examine its actions in the light of history and implored the city counsel to keep the MLK designation. He spoke in a quiet, even, respectful tone from a prepared script."

"There's this elephant in this room, Medina says, "that we try to dance around and walk around and talk around, but if we choose to face it, it will determine where we go, because we *have* to face it. It's not just Zephyrhills problem, it's a national problem. If the street signs were only in the Black neighborhoods, we would have done nothing. It would have been hollow. Metaphorically, we would be saying, stay in your place, and we will stay in ours. I don't think anyone in this room would want to revisit pre-Martin Luther King America. Reversing the street name will gravely affect us. We talked once in this very room about actions which gave this city a black eye. This will be a whammy—I'm not sure it's one we'll ever be able to recover from. There are places and people in this country that are known for hatred. Rodney King, Watts, Selma Alabama. Changing the street name will not end this issue. All it will do is shift the anger and the frustration, from the westside of the railroad tracks to the eastside of the railroad tracks."

The meeting adjourns. All participants go home to different sides of the railroad tracks.

Hanny socks out, as he aways does, "In Pasco County, this is Hanny Perseus, for WKKE radio news."

"Good story," Sebastian Biondi says after the story airs. "Great sound. Could be award material. Proud of you, man."

A day later, Judy, the front desk receptionist, calls Hanny to say, "A woman named Gina White called to explain the difference between stiletto and spike heels. She wears stiletto, she said. She thought you'd like to know and might want to have coffee sometime. She left a number."

Author's Note: The story, "Zephyrhills," is based upon a series of news reports by the author for WMNF in Tampa, Florida, and FSRN in San Francisco, California. Most of the dialogue was transcribed from actual sound taken, from real people gathered by the author, and whose names have been changed. The author was given two awards from the Tampa Bay Association of Black Journalists in 2003 and 2004, for spot reporting and continuing series.

I Danced One Time with Marilyn

It was 1960, and we were both young. The roses were heady that summer, and the ocean was bluer than I had ever seen. Everyone in the neighborhood knew she was a good girl. She called herself by another name back then, before the makeup and the fame, but I knew it would always be her.

She had golden brown and pre-blonde hair. "I'm going to be famous, and successful, and beautiful. Maybe. Someday," she said.

"You already are, with me," I said. There was pollen, and blossoms, and a welling desire in us both.

We played as children do. Ice cream and new music, like colorful balloons. Intellectual talk followed by silliness. The enigma of youth. Explosive petting. Daily tragedy. Champagne and moonlight. We were in love, and we both drank from the cup of dopamine and attraction, like fireflies swarming the summer nights, who light to communicate and to find a mate—she with the scent of rain, and I, as she said, with a hint of woods.

Her mother frowned upon me. There could be an unwanted pregnancy. Before marriage, good girls did not. She kept a careful eye out, and a sharp ear on me.

As teens, we waded into dark waters of sexual attraction. After days of arousal on a crackling plastic-covered couch in her mother's living room, without relief, tired of walking home as an invalid, I resolved to bring up the situation.

"Do you know what epididymal hypertension is?"

And she blushed. Then frowned. "My mother will not allow it."

Her mother was quick to separate us both. My Marilyn went on to college, I did not. I had a taste for the world and traveled. I never saw her again.

We were young then and I was hers. In truth, her name was not Marilyn, but I did not care. I danced one time with Marilyn.

Now, Mannequin

Old man Yossi, again pummeled and knowing he had failed, let himself out of the closet and unbound himself after she left. It was plain that his life was nothing more than a bitter illusion. He stepped into the bedroom and read the letter that was left there, intending to consult his laptop and search for new friends and fresh romance. In the search bar he typed 'contactless love.' It suggested an AI companion.

One of his 'aunties,' the Greek one, had cautioned long ago, "Yossi, the word *hypocrite* comes from the Attic Greek, meaning 'actor,' or 'stage player.' It means to wear many masks—a pretender, a dissembler."

After visiting Broadway for the first time, enjoying Fiddler on the Roof courtesy of one of the aunties affluent clientele, Yossi insisted a life in the theater was for him.

The auntie had added, "Now, wouldn't you be happier as a lawyer or a doctor?"

"But I want to be creative," Yossi had said.

In ancient times, the theater's purpose was to entertain illiterate people. In Roman times, they considered actors as part of an illegitimate profession, similar in status to prostitutes. Most respectable citizens avoided acting, limiting the profession to slaves, or those unfortunates lacking citizenship.

Yossi grew up in a New Jersey whorehouse, with several ethnic aunties—Turkish and Greek and Armenian. The House of Seven Vestibules was a three-story brick building which had formally been a hotel on Port Terminal Boulevard, Bayonne, near the docks. Inside, it was cloaked in dime-store opulence. The draped boudoir-style sitting room downstairs, with overstuffed couches, shouted phony affluence and gaudy excess. The clients were men of substance and common dockworkers both, mainly men in the shipping trade. For an extended time, he was the only young boy on the premises. As a result, the ladies catered to and told him how special he was.

One of his aunties instilled in him the ability to be charming. He came to rely on an amiable and engaging character to affect others completely. "The one who charms others," one Auntie said, likely the Turk, "is the one to get all he wishes." His father, whom he did not know, had been written in as John. It was generally accepted that one of his aunties, most likely the Armenian, was his mother—Jane. As a young boy, in the brothel, he masturbated constantly, and his nickname there was Spunky, for obvious reasons. At seventeen, after years of pleading, the whores pooled their resources and sent him across the river to a NYC acting school.

The aunties expired in turn, leaving him small but heartfelt inheritances, releasing him to fend on his own. He relied on his friends, whom he had grown up with in church and in class, who, having done well, gave him free housing when he needed. They also gave him cash jobs within their various trades which supported his acting career.

He was turning seventy now and whitening, having a slight back problem, and with thin loosening skin which bled at the slightest provocation. He determined that he must do something immediately, otherwise, he'd spend the rest of his life sad, piteous, alone. And it was one dramatic role he did not want to play.

Telling himself his life was *not* a failure, realizing he could no longer be alone, he concluded that his life was damn well worth it and that he deserved better. One day, he determined to take an extreme financial hit and make a large purchase, which he would eventually regret. He called the manufacturer.

"Yes, we can help you," the manufacturer said, soaked in a Yiddish accent. "How tall would you like?"

"I want one just under six feet—"

"How tall are you?"

"Five four. But I like big."

"How big?"

"Big. About one hundred eighty pounds, and blonde. Glam. Like you see in Manchester at night. Big thighs. I like big thighs. And soft in all the right places. And she must have an English accent. From England, London, I think. Stiff upper lip. Opinionated and unflappable. And I want her upright. Proper. An arbiter of propriety when outside and in public. Inside, a whore in bed."

"You're asking a lot. But you've come to the right place. There is a reason we are considered the finest manufacturer of life-size sex dolls in the industry. Our mannequins are all silicone and latex, built with removable body parts for washing. We offer a doll that can open and close eyes as it performs oral. A silicone head and TPE body with a steel frame. Hence the price."

"And reading glasses. And slightly neurotic. I find that a challenge. With shoulder-length blond hair. I find that sexy in bed. With an English accent, as I've said."

"The accent is up to you. She comes to you as a blank slate. Everything you require is what she will be. A strong input is necessary on your part. In essence, your thoughts are hers. But a caution here. Be careful what you wish for."

"Someone with no other purpose or desires than to be there for me."

The manufacturer continued the pitch. "She has fully articulated joints and fingers. But don't you think she would be a bit tall for you? I mean, when you are together, people will be struck with the contrast. An English draft horse and a garden gnome, so to speak." He laughed in an inconsiderate way. The manufacturer did not care if he was insulting. He could afford to be rude. He could detect an immediacy in Yossi's voice. Sex dolls were becoming increasingly popular, especially in China, where the women -to-men ratio was astounding. In Japan, it was worse. More men were passing off mannequins as being real. "In today's society, surrogate women are accepted. But keep in mind, indoctrination is a one-time thing. You cannot change it. She will be whatever you want. It's all up to you. Choose wisely. We cannot be responsible for the results of your initial requirements and your daily input"

"And large pendulous breasts." Yossi said, "She must have large breasts. White breasts. Will she be soft?"

"A fully latex-skinned doll, with a silicone-enhanced body, and articulated joints, as I've said. Arms and legs always ready for you. But not cheap. Three-thousand-two-hundred-dollars-and-nine-cents dressed as risqué as you want. Plus, tax and shipping to your area of course."

Yossi had enough in one of his inheritance accounts. "I'll have one. Send me an order form."

"Very well. You can fill out the form online, include your credit card information, and we'll ship within thirty days."

"Do you offer discounts?"

A cheap one, the manufacturer thought.

And when she arrived, she was as emotional as algebra, and she came with no opinion, and Yossi's complete thoughts. She was exactly what Yossi had expected her to be, and he mistook this for love.

***

For years, in the brothel, Yossi played with little dolls. Animal dolls. Farmer dolls. Soldier dolls. He liked the little girl dolls best of all. His favorite grew old and shabby as he matured, but he did not stop loving her. He spoke with her every day, and she, to him. Her hair became straw-like. Her body became bruised and ugly. The little doll eventually did not look like anything at all anymore, but all little Yossi saw was her beauty. And in his mind, she told him she loved him too. All the criticism from others didn't count, because when one creates magic, nothing else matters. All the whores in the brothel conferred. They took away the dolls when he was nine. It was time for Yossi to stop playing with inanimate objects.

***

Yossi knew many people. He had many acquaintances. People in *'the business.'* Actors need to network. Most of his oldest and ancient friends wanted to write him off as a hopeless romantic, a poser, yes, and cheap, and a bit of a jerk. After moving many years ago to London, most of his oldest friends in New York found him increasingly disingenuous. But, like an old shoe that still fit, they tolerated him, and in a spirit of generosity, generally liked him.

"Don't know you anymore," one friend remarked. "Knew you better in Bayonne."

"What happened to Yossi?" asked another friend downtown. "He's become even more selfish and self-centered since he moved to London. He should have moved to Paris, become more French instead."

"Yes, I agree, much more blunt, like the English who lack all subtlety—no beating around the bush with the French, far less cloak-and-dagger as with the Brits.

"He has an emotional crutch now," a writer friend said. "People change and do not announce it to others."

Yossi was a creature of spontaneity. Whatever ill-thought-out conclusions he had usually came out unhindered from Yossi's mouth. At a restaurant once he said to a friend, who was vulnerable, dentless, and waiting for implants, "What? You don't like the crust?" He applauded. "It's the best part." He gnawed away at a chunk of thick, hard-hulled Greek bread in a most pronounced and flagrant inconsiderate manner. The friend said nothing, noting the insensitivity, dryly thinking, *Your real friends stab you as they face you.*

When he first set off on his acting career, he left Jersey and moved to lower Manhattan, where the rent was controlled, and where all the off-off acting gigs were. After getting nowhere for years, doing showcase work which paid in comps, he eventually opted for London. It was not so affordable, but where, he thought, all the sophistication was. He stayed at a friend's corner flat overlooking the Thames. The friend held the real estate as investment. The house had high ceilings and windows. A strong telescope was handy for viewing ships at harbor and undraped neighbor's windows. One of his favorite views was one middle-aged woman of color who, like clockwork, came home from work at five taking up business with her corset. In the mornings, she struggled to put on her girdle. Trying to escape his Jersey upbringing, he wanted everyone to see him as British—cultured, measured. What came with that was slightly effeminate. A metro-sexual.

Having few friends and even less to do on weekends, he walked the London nightspots, salivating over all the drunk, thick-thigh'd White girls. Those bleach-blonde, mini-skirted women in slutty evening wear strutting their stuff and occasionally falling down in drunken stupor onto the street.

In Indonesia they know how to catch monkeys. Place the bait inside a box with a hole large enough for the monkey's hand. He won't release the food to get his fist back out. This was Yossi's commitment to London and to his acting career.

For over fifty years, Yossi enjoyed calling himself an actor, but looking at his acting, the characterization would be less than stellar. Small parts when he could get them. Few credits. A parasite at times, a sponge, a fawn—he was a person who attempted to gain advantage by flattery, behaving in a servile manner. A charming sycophant.

His first London agent, Mortimer Montague, summed it up before letting him go, "Yossi, you have limited range. You can do Greek or Italian ethnic, or downtown NYC Guido. American South, or even British, is beyond your expertise. You are bad at impressions."

Yossi insisted Mortimer send him out for an audition. The part was for a debonair businessman. "I don't think you're right for the part but go find out for yourself." Yossi borrowed a three-piece suit.

"Thank you for coming," the producer said. "Please read."

What followed was disaster. Yossi got the accent all wrong, did cockney instead of high English. "Ah, yes," the director said. "Thank you for coming. And thank Mortimer as well."

Yossi left the room. "What the hell was that?" asked a script girl.

"Another American expat," a casting agent asked. "A gorilla in a tux. Wait, who's his agent? Montague? He will certainly hear of it."

"A male babushka, should we ever need one. A runt," a camera man said.

"A face perfect for radio," said another.

They all laughed. "Next!" someone shouted.

Later, Mortimer delivered a death knell. "Yossi, you can't sing or dance. Despite having a large ethnic face like a peasant, you try to portray your persona as urbane and debonair. You only come off as smug. An opportunist perpetually waiting to be discovered. And, as all actors are, self-centered, self-congratulatory, and prone to elevating themselves at the expense of others. Constantly self-aggrandizing" Yossi, crushed but still determined, was like a five-year-old looking for importance among whoring adults. And for that, he could thank the Aunties.

***

The first thing Yossi had the mannequin say to him after her unboxing was, "I suppose I'm to be your sex toy, then? What's my name? What will you call me?"

Yossi was thrilled. Not by what she said but by how she said it. The inflection. The accent. Perfect British dryness and a statement-question all in one. No one could hear her. She did not move her mouth. Only Yossi heard in his mind and understood. As his creation, she said exactly what he wanted to hear.

"I think something traditional. An old-fashioned name. Magda, perhaps," he said to the mannequin.

"Sorry?" she said, like she didn't hear. The Brits say *sorry* for everything, even when an apology is unnecessary.

"Magda," Yossi repeated.

"Magda," she said, compliant. And Yossi loved it. From the outset, she had perfect communication skills. What Yossi thought was what Magda said.

"Indeed," Yossi said. He knew the brits enjoy a good *indeed.*

He looked her over for a minute. What he ordered was a drunken, falling-down, Friday night, Liverpool, thick-thigh'd slut woman. She came from the factory dressed in spiked knee-high boots, ass-high skirt, and an extreme push-up bra. Custom-ordered, just for him. And when she walked, she walked heavy-footed and wide-legged, like boatmen, or bouncers, trying to avoid thigh burn. Not close-footed, like dancers and models. The Nutcracker and a perfect pirouette was not her. But that was how Yossi had wanted it. He also walked wide-legged, like a cop or a cowboy, wide-armed to avoid chafing against imaginary side arms. They walked together perfectly, as one.

Yossi felt Magda observing *him* now. She saw what Yossi saw every day in the mirror—a short, dark, stocky man of mixed ethnic strain. Volumes of hair covered his body, including his knuckles and toes. He could not control his right cheek, which twitched upon occasion. His bulbous nose suggested he had some Neanderthal DNA. She came to appreciate his large facial features, thick lips, and bellicose voice—all well-suited for the theater where the distant audience could see and hear well, and love him, Yossi felt, in her own special way.

Yossi was essentially lazy in his career, as capable as a five-star general in a maternity ward, as suited as master gardener in the Mohave, as gifted as a seasoned mariner in the desert. Casting people and the directors who he worked with rarely called him back. His new London agent did the best he could. The studios always required American actors, and low-budget film producers couldn't be that choosy. He could have made something of a career from comic acting, or the laughable ethnic type, instead, he wanted to be seen as dashing, cultured, suave. A Bond type. Yes, *that* Bond. When all his friends came to see him for free on comps, all they saw was Yossi. No magic.

He purchased a GoPro, found a cheap mic, bought a pallet of discarded books in an attempt at soundproofing, and beginning in his sixth decade, he tried reading from Shakespeare for YouTube. The writer friend, trained to notice, said he was without talent. He created nothing. He relied on the writers to do the art. For a time, his voice-overs paid the bills. He considered himself an artist but wasn't. His expertise was in reading what writers had written. He invented what he thought was a clean American Midwestern accent for this work. Everyone familiar with accents wondered exactly where in the Midwest it could have come from.

Yossi loved good cigars, expensive whiskey, and fireplaces on yachts owned by whomever he could fawn over because of their wealth. He liked to think his love of cigars included him into a select group of exclusive club members. This was his homage toward British royalty. And Shakespeare. He never tired of telling everyone, "Shakespeare is my favorite author."

***

"So, what's now, mister? Having problems with women still, I suppose?" Brick's comment came with a snort. Brick was the swarthy Russian cook and the alcoholic in the whorehouse who still lived in the basement of the building where Yossi had grown up. He drove an old Mercedes. Some said he still had mob connections. He watched Yossi as he grew, considered him a bum, and said so. Someone without aspirations. Someone who relied upon his Aunties for support.

He was drinking vodka straight from the bottle when Yossi came to see him two weeks before the mannequin arrived.

"I'm afraid so," Yossi admitted.

Throughout his young adulthood, and after leaving the brothel, Yossi would visit Brick. Brick jumped ship from a Greek freighter in NY harbor in 1950. He got his nickname after the oblong copper coffeemaker, a *Briki,* found in Greek coffee houses. Brick pronounced his name, *Breik.* He rolled his R's. He was fond of saying, *I'm Breik, not Greek.* He was very careful with money, salivated when counting it. He weighed out emotion like a grocer protecting every ounce.

"Still the French girl? The one with her bowling-pin figure and bad teeth like you told me?" Brick, xenophobic and from the old country, a Communist, operated with a perfect memory.

In the sixties, for a time, Yossi had been with the French girl. He had luxuriated in her cellulite bottom and her thick thighs she had from eating all that cheese. Sad, she had said, about all his lost-love stories. Conversations with her, usually bland, were mostly about food. Her English was limited, and Yossi's French halting. She had a small bank account. He would insist she pay her fair share. She had returned to her country broke and angry, after Yossi's repeated insensitive remarks about her figure and teeth. He had thought he was tactful. She had dumped him after she had exhausted her meager savings. She had called him cheap in the end, too noncommittal, and they broke. Her adventure in Manhattan over, Yossi was alone again.

"Oh, yes, but that was a long time ago," Yossi said. "You know, soon after that, I was very much in love with Tania, the Italian."

"She was older than you, and with a full figure kind of way, you said."

"She wore garters and dark stockings, Sophia-style, to entice." Yossi gave Brick his most polished look, attempting a Cary Grant.

"Ah, yes," Brick waxed, eyes glassing over. "Sophia Loren, now *that* was a woman."

"She liked to dine out every night, have coffee all day, buy nice shoes." Yossi looked around at the hand-me-down furniture in the whorehouse basement, so familiar and comfortable.

"She didn't like your long talking about her sagging breasts, her flat bottom, and her varicose veins, if I remember you saying." Brick offered Yossi. who refused, then took a long pull from his vodka. "You never have picked women for the right reasons, my boy."

The Italian dumped him as well, saying he was too noncommittal, too self-important, and too tight with complements and money. Yossi, left alone and abandoned, had been crushed once again. And there were others. Cold, Northern White women. Yossi loved the attitude, loved the stoic which originated from the Greek. Most likely the philosophy was imported from Northern Europe in ancient times. He also identified with New York, forever a collection of ethnicities. Stand on a corner, and the whole world passes you by. One of the perks of being a male actor, or a dancer, was the amount of gay people in the arts. Perfect dating for a straight man.

German girls could destroy with a simple glance. For Yossi, a few of them in succession. Swedish women stayed for a drink—or ten. English women were the pisspots of Europe. He liked them all right, for most were financially independent, distant, and shied away from long-term commitments. One had dumped him, saying he was too needy. Another had thought him too short. The German loved Kant, a rational empiric. She had seen no reason to be with him.

"Ah, yes," said Brick, "with the Germans, what you see is what you get. No bullshit." He said it *bool-sheet.* He waxed philosophic and misogynistic. "Some women are tough. Others pretend to be, so to protect themselves more fully. There is a difference between beer-swilling Germans and the silly English. Stick with wine drinkers. And do not discount the whiskey drinking Americans, who all want children." He fingered his Stoli like it was a lover.

Yossi felt all women too expensive to keep. Some of these women had serious relationships with food. And to take them out for drinks proved extremely expensive. He did not relish the responsibility. It was comforting to have someone to go home to, but Yossi liked to keep accounts straight. A roll of toilet tissue, sheet by sheet, lasted a month. Somewhere in his possessions were the first single, five, ten, and twenty dollar bills he had ever encountered.

"What is my problem? Why can't I have a long-term relationship? Why can't I be like everyone else, Brick?

If you want admiration, get yourself a dog. If you want adulation, call yourself an actor.

"You never had a pet, did you?"

"No," Yossi admitted.

***

After a few months as an item, Yossi introduced Magda to his friend, a playwright. Across the restaurant table, in conversation, the writer revealed his new dialogue-heavy screenplay he'd been working on, about a group of drunk women boldly discussing male genitalia, in the way women in a close-knit private group might. At times, the writer excelled at producing content which would provoke. The writer was proud of his ability to pen disparate dialogue. Yossi always maintained his love of Shakespeare. Yossi had Magda react as he saw fit, in typical British fashion. He had her freeze, indignant.

Before the mannequin, Yossi felt for others. Now, with Magda, all empathy for others was completely gone. "This is not a topic you should mention at a dinner table," he said, affronted, defending his proper English mannequin's sensibilities. "I'll thank you to take your smut talk elsewhere." The writer did not defend, noting the counterfeit, disingenuous, and affected attitude. He was not a fan of Shakespeare. After dinner, the writer rose and pulled Marsha into an extended full-body hug. The mannequin did not resist. Unable to stop it, Yossi stood there and looked like he was about to cry.

Like a jailer, Yossi held onto non-existent keys to locks. From an early age, he decided he would be better off appearing as a *good guy*. One woman he had been in love with, a German psychologist in Greece, had summed it up. "Men with unresolved and unhealed inner-child issues often become insecure 'nice guys' with deep frustration and unexplained reactivity, feeling like, no matter what they do for their partners, it is never good enough." She paused as

Yossi, listening, slowly reduced into a thick, putrid, hepatitis-colored liquid right before her. "You can excuse fear, loathing, and ignorance when you grow up in an upbringing with constant pressure to be better, I suppose, but grow out of it, man." It was the Aunties again. And the net result for Yossi was misplaced egotism.

But trouble does not limit itself to censorship. After about a year, Magda complained in dissatisfaction, or did it come from Yossi's own discontent, "Why couldn't you order me thinner? Why do you want me this way? My only purpose is to please you. And let's talk about your pathetic infant desires. You could have ordered a doctor, or a physicist, or even a mother. You could have had a mother with a child. You *bloody* bastard."

Yossi, refusing to part with keys to emotional locks which existed only in his mind, relying on solutions to problems long-forgotten, looked at her with painful eyes of bleeding guilt. "I wanted a mate. I was so lonely."

"Rubbish," she said flatly, forcing herself to step outside her British comfort zone. "I am not amused. I want to be sent back to the manufacturer." she said, French-like, with the perfect air of dry defiance that a server adopts in announcing that the cheapest-priced drink in the wine list had finished. She gave him a steely, stone-faced look, and Yossi shuddered. Why was she speaking suddenly with a French accent?

In a moment of extreme clarity, what Yossi saw in front of him now was a big, tall, white-breasted woman, a shopkeeper's daughter, posing elite, with large expansive feet, a transplant Londoner. Yes, she could be reserved in mixed company, human or mannequin, both. Exactly what Yossi wanted. Never speaking in public, she spoke only to him. Only Yossi heard her. Conservative, reserved—she did not approve of kissing or hugging in public. And Yossi was good with that. It was how Yossi wanted her—British conservative, stiff-lipped and opinionated, with cold, disguised motives, and he came to regret it. But, daily, he loved it. It made him want her even more. He loved the abuse.

"I've been waiting for someone like you for a very long time," Yossi pleaded. "Please don't spoil it for me. I need you."

Take your needs and dispose of them. Be a man. Now, toss off."

It wasn't the first time he had put her in the closet and left her there for days. Later, tired and done with vindication, he let her out. He was feeling lonely and done with masturbation.

"Can we make love tonight?" he asked, even though lately he'd been having difficulties.

"No. I'm not in the mood. And you're no good."

That hurt. "Are you angry with me?"

"Yes."

"Why? What did I do?"

"Do you remember the first time you locked me in the closet when you didn't like what I said about your manhood? You bleeding wanker. And the other time, when the neighbor, the Frenchman, barged in unexpectedly. You put me in the other room. You didn't want him to see me half naked in decolletage and to desire me, now, did you? The Frenchman asked to borrow a cup of something. And when you went into the kitchen to get it for him. He fondled my breasts and tested my rear."

"What? Why is this the first time I'm hearing about this?"

It wasn't. Yossi had suspected at the time. Something later in the Frenchman's face. Yossi projected upon Magda his wretched demons.

"You secretly want other men to want me, don't you? And when they do, you act so destroyed. You are so jealous. The sign of a weak man. I know you've always coveted your friends' wives, haven't you?"

Yossi was painfully aware of his cheap indiscretions. He feared payback. Kharma. What goes around comes around. Yossi was terrified of being blatantly cuckolded, as he had cuckolded others. As much as he acted the Lothario, he felt sexually inadequate. He needed to overcompensate and had cuckolded his friends before, and that made him feel superior. He needed to assert his manhood. At least one acquaintance spoke of him as an eater of carrion, circling above in want, waiting to feed on dying relationships.

"It's only because I need you so much," he said to Magda. "I'm afraid of losing you."

For the rest of the day, she gave him the silent treatment, which he hated more than anything else. He was constantly seeking reassurance from her, even when he projected his thoughts onto her. He never had safe space as a boy to claim any truth and assert a strong sense of self.

The next day he propped her up on a stool in a corner of the kitchen, hands in lap, and locked the front door behind him. From the hallway, where she couldn't hear, he called the manufacturer. The Frenchman next door, hearing him exit, scaled the partition between their balconies. The boxed red wine Yossi drank, on the counter, sickened him. The domestic American cheese in the refrigerator, appalled him. There was no butter to be found. Sliced white bread in the cupboard began to mold.

"Wait for me, my darling," the neighbor said to the mannequin in French, then kissed her open mouth, and took her from behind in quick fashion while Yossi complained into the phone outside.

"Why is she so cruel to me?" Yossi asked the manufacturer.

"It is what you ordered."

"She complains all the time. And I'm not quite sure she is faithful to me."

"You wanted fifty, you got menopausal." Yossi knew nothing about menopause, but he did know neurotic. "You asked for a whore. It's what you got."

"I want you to change whatever neural networks I've given her."

"Not possible. You were warned. You did not choose wisely." The manufacturer paused. "There is a way, but you will pay again the same price as the original."

"What do you mean?"

"Change everything. Modify to something more suitable. Perhaps a small, thin, Japanese brunette this time."

"I can't do Asian, and I will *not* pay again."

"So be it. If you like, I will connect you with our in-house counselor and customer service specialist." Which he did.

"Did you play with dolls as a child? Imaginary entities?" The 'psychologist' paused. Yossi said nothing. "Well then, you should know that what you pretend is what you get. Cosplay. If you want the mannequin to behave differently, well then, you should look to yourself, perhaps. Y*our* input drives the Mannequin. Look as well into licensed therapy. We can refer you for free."

Yossi was not feeling strong. He had tired of confronting his malignant demons. And he refused to spend any more unnecessary money.

After three days of apologizing to Magda, she relented, and they attempted love. Yossi luxuriated in folds of latex skin and silicone breasts and her large expansive rear. He did not have difficulty with climax. Reaffirmation after humiliation, for Yossi, was an exquisite delight.

***

On their second anniversary, Yossi took Magda to the French restaurant at the end of the street of their three-story flat. He dressed her in a plain black tent dress, one which kept her large white breasts and expansive buttocks sheathed. He dressed her like this every time they went out in public. Only he knew what she wore underneath. Beneath the plain black dress, he had her in the most wicked outfit he could order online.

The waiter from the apartment adjacent to Yossi noticed them immediately. Waiters notice everything. Something about the nine-inch, ankle-strap, red heels she wore along with the tent dress, giving her completely away.

Yossi had fastened a Velcro attachment to their opposite ankles—his right, her left. With his hand across her waist, and with her arm around his shoulder, they walked in-step, as lovers do. Gentlemanlike, Yossi placed her in her seat. She sat at the table, complacent, hands in lap. Yossi ordered a Chateau Briand, with roasted asparagus on the side. "And a house salad. With Russian dressing, please."

The waiter from the apartment next to Yossi furrowed his brow. Russian dressing in a French restaurant. "And for madam?" The waiter was sure this was a man who deserved cuckolding. She never seemed to age. She sat at the table next to Yossi, frozen in vacant expression. Vacant as a mannequin, open-mouthed as if in expectation, a bit of pink tongue showing. The waiter struggled to maintain.

"Nothing, thank you."

The waiter, without pretense, visibly appreciated her breasts, and her thick thighs in the black dress, openly sneered at Yossi, wet his lips like he had finished enjoying a succulent coq au vin, and slightly nodded. Yes, he had her on multiple occasions, and he had come to believe it was *he* who owned her.

"And to drink?" the waiter asked. He knew her. He knew her as a woman who would accept a man's faults, love him unreservedly, not talk back, enjoy being manhandled, and be what all Frenchmen wanted—a whore in bed. When she was his, he would rename her Myra.

Yossi ordered, "House wine, thank you, and two glasses."

Stone-faced, the waiter returned with a carafe of red wine and two glasses. Yossi leaned forward and articulated her fingers around the wineglass stem, then bent near to her ear and whispered, "Open your mouth a bit more." He helped her do that, giving the waiter a dark look.

After the waiter left the table, Yossi's mannequin said, "Why are my thighs always double-sized every time I sit down? That's what you ordered, isn't it? What do you think I am, one of your Turkish harem girls? I am English. I am entitled. I deserve better."

She was in high pitch now. Only Yossi heard. He did not like it when she was like that. He could do little to control her or himself—or his projections on her. "Why do you always keep me in high uplift, with loose bra straps, so when we walk around London, I bounce all over? Like a cheap courtesan," she spat. "And why did you order me so heavy? Do you think

I enjoy carting my weight around like a cow? You think of me like a date rape, a common whore, a drunk slut on a Friday night, don't you?"

"But that's what I like. You are here only for me," Yossi defended. He was in uncharacteristic punching mode, brothel style. The Frenchman was beginning to get to him. "And that's what *you* should like, you friggin' cow," he said, to hurt. He immediately regretted it.

She, of late, was searching like a grapevine tendril, curling, searching the distance, reaching for a place to attach. She knew she had been made to be about fifty, and menopausal. Yossi didn't know why he made her act that way. And Yossi let her do that, unencumbered. He felt compelled, however wrong he knew it was, to control and direct her that way. He always regretted it in the end.

"Why do you always treat me like I'm here for only one reason? Just here for a good shag?" she asked.

Yossi gave her a hurt look. He knew he would be punished now. It was a look of complete devastation. One she'd come to despise him for his weakness. It was hang-dog. Aggrieved, crushed, distressed, mauled and wounded.

"Please don't look at me with that hurt droopy face. You need to be a bit more thick skinned," she said, as if she were the only one to do that. "You want to be more British. Don't you? You moved to London to become more British, didn't you? Isn't *that* right? Yes or no?"

"But I love you, Magda. Please. I don't want to be in trouble with you. I'll do better in the future, I promise."

"You love me? You tell me what that means, and I will believe you."

Yossi gave her his most practiced hurt look.

Magda now came out with a comment Yossi hated most. Where it came from, he did not fully understand. "Actors," she said, "are inherently stupid people. Alfred Hitchcock called them cattle, and Otto Premenger said the dumber they are, the better. Capote also made the statement that all actors were stupid."

Yossi refrained from answering, continued the hurt look, remained submissive throughout dinner. The waiter returned repeatedly, with a fire in his eyes that Yossi noticed and did not like, speaking only in French now, attending to their needs and becoming increasingly attentive to Magda. At one point, Yossi thought he heard Magda say to the waiter, in French, "Merci, Mon Cher."

***

Close to their third anniversary, it was Magda's turn to force Yossi to remain in the closet, alone. She was in complete control now. She required him to wear a blindfold and a ball gag, which he administered himself. He self-bound his hands and feet. He stayed there for one full day, punished. When he let himself out, Magda was gone. On the bed was a note, in a male French hand. It read, *You are old. You are inflexible. You are cheap, and you smell of urine. The flesh hangs from your bones. You are an incompetent lover. I regret having met you. I will never die. I am French now. You will die, I will live. Au Revoir, Myra.*

Yossi went into the kitchen to make himself a tuna fish sandwich and then ate it. Outside, from his window, attached to a lamp pole, was a sign which read, LOST DOG. There was a telephone number. He reentered the closet where he sat, longing for admiration, missing his mannequin, and doing his penance. Yossi was once again alone. Sad, piteous, and alone.

Damn Some Characters

Sometimes I get up in the middle of the night, suffering too many thoughts. It is 4a.m, too early for coffee, but I stumble out of bed and make it, anyway. Life is too short to spend time sleeping.

"Don't you have anything better to do?" the new character says to me. "What *is* this?" He does not have a name yet, but I know him to be an actor. And I know actors. This one is a spoiled little fictional bastard who has infiltrated my mind as I prepare to write a new story.

My characters often talk to me asking for certain assurances, to set parameters and to vent any insecurities. Writers always hear from their fictional characters. Some writers can be kind, others not, as the subject matter dictates.

"I give you no guarantees," I say to the actor who tries to pull a guilt trip on me. I begin to know this character, and he begins to annoy me. "And to be clear, I can be scathing."

"Don't be scathing," he says.

"I'll be as delicate as a burly Welsh miner, carrying a large pickaxe, confronting a fat golden vein," I assure him.

"What are you doing this for?" he wants to know.

"First off, you do not end a sentence with a preposition. And second, I do not answer to my fictional characters. You serve at my pleasure, exist only on paper or in electronic form, and only because I allow you to."

"Who do you think you are?" he asks, incensed.

"A writer," I answer. "Who is that woman beside you now?"

"I don't know, but she says she despises you, and if she doesn't like what you write about her, she'll sue."

"Why can't I hear her?"

"I don't know. She's from somewhere in the UK, I think. And if you write about me, I won't read it."

"Let me get this straight," I say. "One of my characters, the main character in my next work, says he won't read what I write. The other says she'll sue me. Is that correct?"

"Yes. So, write what you want. I don't have to read it, Mr. Shakespeare."

"Okay. You both need to understand something. You both are fictional characters. Read the disclaimer at the beginning of the book. No one you know, living or dead? And be forewarned, I could force you both to fall off a cliff, or have you suffer incredibly intense pain, and kill you both at any time. So, know it."

And so, armed in advance with two recalcitrant characters, I sit down this early morning with my coffee to write the next epic story. It is called … well, you know what it is called.

The Longest Road in the World to Walk

That early morning, I stopped for a stranger walking alone along a highway many miles from anywhere. "Do you need help?" My purpose in life was to document my time and to witness those things that cross my path. I was an investigative reporter.

"No, thank you. But thanks for asking."

The longest road in the world to walk, is from Cape Town South Africa, to Magadan Russia. No need for planes or boats. There are bridges.

"Where are you going?" He carried little, and there was nothing around.

"Sorry, I can't talk now. That dog is following me."

I looked. There was no dog. "What dog is that?"

"The red one behind me. I brought him up from a pup." He looked at me like he wondered whether he should talk to me. "We lived in the city then. We'd take long walks at night. I taught him to heel, because a lot happens in the city."

"What city was that?"

"Why, Cape Town. Is there any other?"

"Well, there are a few. What's your name, friend?"

"Mathew. What's yours?"

"I'm Rachel. I write. My apologies for all the questions. Writers do that."

"A good dog," he continued, "a setter. When we crossed the street, I allowed him to race down the block to the next corner, where he'd stop and wait for me to cross him, in Cape Town city. Later, we moved to the country where we both were free to roam. We were both happier then. He used to love riding in the back of the truck, with his face in the wind. In the village, he knew to stay in the back like I told him. He'd only move if it was hot and there was some shade in a nearby doorway. An excellent dog."

It was hot. We moved under some shade. "So, where are you going now? You say you came from Cape Town. Do you know how far you've walked already?"

"Not quite sure—just following the road here—been through fourteen pairs of shoes. The dog knows, though." He laughed and pointed rearward with his head.

"The dog behind you," I said, even though there was nothing.

"Yes."

"But I see no dog."

"*That* is your problem."

The longest road in the world to walk, is 22,387 kilometers—13,911 miles—and it takes 4,492 hours to travel.

"Do you know you are in Egypt? Cape Town is at least seven thousand miles from here."

"If you say so." He whistled, transferring his gaze downward. "Good dog." He brought a bandana from his pocket, mopped his head, then motioned, as if to lovingly stroke the dog. "And then one day," he said as if he'd already been on the subject, "the whole world collapsed and I was forced to go back to the city. I gave the dog to a man who had acreage and a pickup truck. I lost the wife then, the farm, the dog, all of it. I will never forget the look on the dogs face, looking me straight in the eye, when I told him to get into that man's truck. He jumped right in because I told him. He tethered him. Couldn't move. He asked with his eyes. Why? He didn't understand. I couldn't tell him. You know, they say that when a man's dog sees his master dead, he understands, and mourns."

The longest road in the world to walk, takes 187 days walking nonstop, or 561 days walking 8 hours a day. Along the route, you pass through 17 countries, six time zones and all seasons of the year.

"And then, you see, one day, those who tear up the earth for profit came for my land. It's called rape. After some years, I came looking for my dog. The land was changed. The mining company Oneida cut a road on the back side of the ridge, sneaked down into the old homesite, culverted the creek—used that old apple orchard with the waterfall as a staging area for deep mining and logging. They ruined it. And they didn't care. When we lived there back then, I used to call the dog, big loud calls, echoing down the valley. Wherever he was, he'd come running for his ride into town. Now I got him back."

That light, the last light slanting at sunset hours, low casting reddish, where one takes time to reflect on what you have done with your day, what the new mornings light brings, and what one can expect from the night.

We camped out and we sat around a small fire. I shared some dried food which I had in the car that I had soaked in water and boiled. At times, he made noises like he was talking to the dog, coming from his heart, lonely sounds, like he knew that dog had made after he had abandoned it, when he had returned to the city. He didn't want the dog to suffer. After so many years, the dog must have died, heartbroken, like him. He told me, without words, that there were moments when he was at peace with his unhappiness. He understood it. It was apparent and clear, and he accepted it as the net result of what he had become, without thought of harming himself.

"It took me so many years to find that dog, and here he is." He studied his feet. "I died you know. And so did he."

In the morning, he was gone, not to be seen. I spotted something red and gaunt in the far distance, chasing behind something not there.

***

The sheep will spend its entire life fearing the wolf, only to be eaten by the shepherd. The twisted tree lives out its life. The straight tree ends up a board.

The longest road in the world to walk is sometimes the only road to walk to escape your guilt.

www.ingramcontent.com/pod-product-compliance
Lightning Source LLC
LaVergne TN
LVHW090528110826
845146LV00003B/1022

* 9 7 9 8 9 9 5 3 2 3 0 0 6 *